MURDER IN
BLACK AND WHITE

Other books by Loretta Jackson and Vickie Britton:

Arctic Legacy

The Luck of the Draw Western Series
The Devil's Game
The Fifth Ace
The Wild Card

MURDER IN
BLACK AND WHITE

•

Loretta Jackson
and Vickie Britton

AVALON BOOKS
NEW YORK

Published by Avalon Books,
an imprint of Thomas Bouregy & Co., Inc.
160 Madison Avenue, New York, NY 10016

Library of Congress Cataloging-in-Publication Data
Jackson, Loretta.
    Murder in black and white / Loretta Jackson and Vickie Britton.
        p.   cm.
    ISBN 978-0-8034-7719-3
    1. Sheriffs—Fiction.   2. Photographers—Fiction.
3. Secrets—Fiction.   4. Small cities—Fiction.   I. Britton,
Vickie.   II. Title.
    PS3560.A224M87 2011
    813'.54—dc22

                                                    2010031115

PRINTED IN THE UNITED STATES OF AMERICA
ON ACID-FREE PAPER
BY HADDON CRAFTSMEN, BLOOMSBURG, PENNSYLVANIA

Chapter One

Sheriff Jeff McQuede entered the huge exhibit hall, empty except for the giant black bear that guarded the Coal County Museum's entrance. He paused a moment before the sign that read OPEN HOUSE TODAY 7 P.M., then forged on, passing arrowheads and pottery and dinosaur bones until he reached the other end of the room and the long, dim corridor that led to Loris Conner's office.

Nearing her door, he slowed his pace and straightened his turquoise bolo tie. As he did, he was assailed by a strong scent of spice and knew he had overdone it on the aftershave lotion. He hesitated, feeling as self-conscious as an awkward teenager, not a man in his early forties.

The openings he had carefully rehearsed still played in his head. *I was just passing through and thought we might catch a bite of dinner when you get off work. . . . Loris, I was wondering if you've seen that movie down at the Grand.* All wrong now. His hopes had been dashed by the news of the open house, for tonight she would be slated to work late.

McQuede quickly revised his plans. He would ask if she was busy Sunday. If she agreed to see him, he'd take her to that fancy steakhouse that had just opened on the edge of town. If he acted quickly, he could catch Loris before any visitors appeared so he would not have to pose his question before an audience.

As McQuede made his way forward, he drew courage from the old cliché "Faint heart never won fair lady." He had lifted his hand to knock when he became aware of the turning doorknob. He quickly stepped back against the wall, and remained there unseen. Pale, honey blond hair in an upsweep, heels making a busy, clicking sound, Loris looked neither left nor right as she bustled off toward the main exhibit room. Someone met her there, for he could hear the sound of voices.

He'd have to change his strategy, wait and waylay Loris on her return. Biding his time, McQuede paused to study the framed pictures that lined the walls, a new addition that must have come from the old high school, scheduled for demolition in a matter of days. Classes from Black Mountain Pass High hung neatly, rows of photos in black and white. Only about twelve years were represented, skipping randomly from 1955 to 1988.

McQuede, who had gone to the rival school in Durmont, didn't know many of the students, but he knew Loris Conner had graduated from Black Mountain Pass. He scanned the 1988 class, which would be about the right year, searching for her face, as he often found himself doing at the civic meetings they were both duty-bound by their jobs to attend. He quickly located Loris among the thirty or so students, her eyes serious and wistful behind the large-framed glasses that were the style at the time, the kind that made him think of another cliché, "Boys never make passes at girls who wear glasses."

Of course that wasn't true in Loris' case, for she had the classic features of a Greek beauty. She had looked shy then, but now carried herself with poise, grace, and self-confidence.

He recognized a couple of her classmates, Fredrick Preston, of the old-money Prestons, and Everett Ganner, his chin cleft and prominent, who for years had been principal of the soon-to-be demolished school.

McQuede had started to turn away when a photo at the bottom caught his attention. Beneath the likeness of a brooding, dark-haired boy named Jerome Slade, someone long ago had neatly printed the words *never graduated*.

McQuede leaned closer, studying the face of a youth with longish hair and dark-browed, piercing eyes that put him in mind of the old film *Rebel Without a Cause* and its hero, James Dean. McQuede wondered if this Jerome had dropped out late, after the class pictures had already been taken, or if his grades had been too bad to allow him the benefit of a diploma. Whatever the case, instead of being left out, he had been included, but with this notation to set the record straight. It seemed sad now, this remark, like an epitaph. No matter what else he might have been or done, this penned announcement seemed to separate him from the others, pointing out this single failure to the world for all eternity.

McQuede wondered briefly what had happened to him. Maybe he had run off to enlist, maybe he had taken off for California prior to graduation, as the rebellious were known to do. But as he stood there, an eerie feeling gripped him. A sense of heaviness and sorrow that for no reason at all made him think this surly, unhappy-looking boy had found an early grave.

Behind him the back door of the museum rattled, jarring him from his gloomy thoughts. The high school principal, Everett Ganner, burst into the corridor, as if, more than two decades later, he had just materialized from his class photo. He wore a casual sports jacket and lugged a heavy box. His face still looked boyish, broad and smiling, his thick brown hair always slightly ruffled.

He laughed heartily. "What's our renowned sheriff doing in a peaceful place like this?" He drew to a stop. "Do you know where I can find Loris? I've brought some more items for the open house this evening."

McQuede indicated the exhibit area. "How's the move going? Must be quite a job, changing over to that big, consolidated school."

"We'll be holding classes at the old place until the end of this week," Ganner said.

Ganner passed him, and McQuede ambled closer to the main hall. Loris, near the stuffed bear, stood talking to Fredrick Preston III. Preston, with his sharp-featured, intent face, hadn't changed much in the past twenty-odd years, though he now sported a black, pencil-thin mustache, probably to distinguish him from his look-alike father.

His grandfather had founded Preston Coal, and this spoiled grandson had always taken advantage of that fact. He stood very close to Loris. Preston, divorced, was probably looking for another wife, McQuede thought sourly.

McQuede watched as Preston leaned even closer to Loris as if to share some secret. They both began laughing. If McQuede had chosen to join them, the laughing would have abruptly stopped. McQuede knew the reason why, for his presence often brought with it reticence and even fear. McQuede had the same silvery eyes and rugged features of his namesake, his great-uncle, who had been one of the territory's most feared lawman.

Ev Ganner, who had been standing as silent as McQuede, now strode forward, eyes for no one but Loris, his loud voice booming across the room. His words were lost to McQuede, for a group of community-spirited helpers, dressed in sweatshirts and jeans, began streaming in through the main entrance. No chance of catching Loris alone now. McQuede had hesitated . . . and lost.

He had no desire to join the group, to make an attempt at idle chitchat, or to compete for Loris' attention with Black Mountain's two most eligible bachelors. He was and would always be just a down-to-earth, rough-edged sheriff. She would probably have turned him down anyway.

"Sheriff McQuede? Loris Conner."

Her voice, so strained and serious, caught him off guard. His hand tightened on the phone. Embarrassment filled him as he wondered if she had noticed his hasty exit yesterday from the museum. Or maybe Ev Ganner had mentioned running into him. He felt trapped, busted, like some criminal caught casing a joint. Was she going to demand some kind of explanation of why he had been lurking around the museum without even saying hello? How would he ever explain that the fearless sheriff of Coal County had wanted to ask her out on a date and had at the last minute lost his nerve?

"I hope you don't mind my phoning you at home."

"Not at all. I was in Black Mountain Pass yesterday. I stopped by the museum, but you were busy, and I didn't stay long."

"I don't want to talk to anyone but you. Something very strange has happened, Jeff. At the museum."

So this was strictly business. Still, he couldn't help noticing that she had called him Jeff. "Better tell me about it."

"I found the back door broken when I arrived at work this morning. But the odd part is, nothing seems to be missing."

"What happened to your security system?"

"It's kind of a makeshift affair with a switch that turns it on and off. I activated it when I closed the museum last night, but it was off this morning."

"I'll drive over and take a look around."

Loris was waiting for him in the parking lot, looking both businesslike and attractive in a pale blue skirt and blouse, cream-colored jacket, and matching heels.

"When I came in this morning at ten-thirty, I noticed the back door was slightly ajar." Loris led him to the same exit he had slipped out of last night, where splinters of wood encircled a broken lock.

McQuede surveyed the damage, then followed her into the museum, which looked the same as yesterday. His gaze roved over the precious Native American collection, the expensive pottery. Nothing appeared to be disturbed. Most surprising of all, valuable guns, quick targets for robbers, remained intact behind glass-encased displays.

"Why don't you check your files? See if any papers are missing."

"I didn't think anyone was in my office, but I'll check again." She scurried away.

After a while, satisfied that nothing had been stolen, McQuede headed down the corridor to join her. As he did, his gaze fell to the line of class photos. He started past, then turned back, startled. The frame containing the Class of 1988 was gone.

As Loris approached, he asked, "Did you move any of these pictures?"

"No."

"One is missing."

"Why, you're right," she said with amazement. "My class—l988. I hung it there myself." Her gaze met his, disbelief present in her wide, hazel eyes. "With all the items of value in here, who would break in to steal some old class photo?"

"It's not the crime of the century, is it? I'll file a report, but don't be expecting to get that class picture back." He started to the door. "Better see to that lock."

"I've already called a repairman. Jeff, wait."

He turned back. The puzzled look had vanished from her eyes, replaced with a glint of realization. "If you have time for lunch, my assistant will watch the museum. I think I might know who stole that picture."

Chapter Two

McQuede couldn't help but feel a sense of elation. He was having his date with the pretty museum curator, after all. Of course, there wouldn't be any romantic music or candlelit tables, not at Mom and Pop's Café, which looked like a relic from the '50s, complete with checkered table-cloths, vinyl seats, and strong, bitter coffee. But he wasn't going to complain. Loris and he were having lunch, and what's more, she had been the one to ask him out.

He felt relaxed and happy, and why not? The theft of a class picture was hardly a matter of life and death. He soon found, though, that Loris didn't share his mood.

She looked distractedly at the menu, then removed her glasses and gazed directly at him, her hazel eyes appearing more green than brown. Without her glasses she looked startlingly different, perfectly flawless, a Greek statue even further out of reach. For a moment, he imagined her with her hair hanging loose and free.

"I really don't know what to do about this. I suppose I

should file a report with our head office in Cheyenne, but the picture was nothing valuable, and not even officially part of our collection."

"Was this one of the items Ev Ganner donated to the museum?"

"No, the journalism teacher, Bruce Fenton, brought them over, after he found them in the storage room. Even though the collection wasn't complete, I hung them in the hallway, thinking the locals might enjoy them. I hadn't even logged them in yet, so I'd have a hard time proving that the photo ever existed."

"We have witnesses, remember?" McQuede said lightly. "You and me." McQuede, turning serious, leaned forward. "You said you might know who took the picture. You must have noticed someone around that area last night."

Loris now seemed uncertain. "We had such a large crowd. I owe that to Fredrick Preston, I suppose. He's always the one responsible for bringing in all of our big donors."

"Black Mountain Pass would no doubt wither away without him," McQuede said, then rebuked himself for the edge of jealousy that had probably crept into his voice. "Loris," he went on quickly, "I noticed one photo in particular of a boy named Jerome Slade. Beneath his picture someone had printed *never graduated.*"

She reacted with a sudden sadness. "The senior class pictures were taken about a month before graduation. But Jerome never completed his finals."

"Why not?"

Loris looked away from him, as if to shield the darkness that had crept into her eyes. "He simply . . . disappeared."

McQuede's brows furrowed. "I don't recall there ever being anything in the papers about a missing student."

"Oh, there wouldn't have been. He had already turned eighteen, and he had reason enough for leaving here." Her gaze switched back to him. "Jerome wasn't a bad person, one of those guys who are all caught up in their music, their dreams of being a big star. A little wild, maybe, but not a pipe dreamer, for he had enough talent to really make it."

The darkness had not left her eyes. He could tell by the tone of her voice that she had liked Jerome, maybe even cared about him in a romantic way. He wondered if her first love had been Jerome Slade, her first kiss. Here he was, jealous again, this time of a man missing since 1988.

"For a long time after he . . . left . . . I'd be listening to the radio and thinking maybe someday I'd hear one of his songs. I never did, though."

Just another young man with big dreams who ended up behind the counter of a convenience store, McQuede thought, but said nothing. Still, it seemed odd that he had never touched base with anyone in his hometown.

"In our junior year, Jerome, Everett, Bruce, and an older boy, Harlan, started a band. Jerome had high hopes for it, called it *Orion*. By the time they were seniors, they had contacted a manager who Jerome claimed was going to 'make their names known all over the world.'" She looked at him sadly.

"But that's not what I want to talk to you about. I think I know who stole the picture." She took a deep breath. "Jerome's father, Bernard Slade, showed up at the museum last night. Drunk. I was afraid he might cause a scene, that

I'd have to ask him to leave, but he didn't cause any trouble."

"But you believe he returned, broke in, and stole his son's picture? That doesn't make much sense. You'd probably have run him off a copy if he'd asked for one."

"Mr. Slade doesn't always make sense."

"Maybe he saw what was written under Jerome's name about his never graduating and decided he didn't want that announcement on display. A family pride thing."

"You don't know Bernard Slade."

As a matter of fact, McQuede did know him. He'd been a guest in McQuede's jail numerous times. Not a bad fellow when he was sober, but he was one mean drunk.

Loris hesitated a moment, then added in a lower tone, "Every so often Jerome would show up at school with cuts and bruises. He'd make jokes about them, but I always thought I knew the truth—Jerome was afraid of his father. Jeff, if Bernard Slade is the one who took the picture, it wasn't for any sentimental reason."

McQuede didn't spend much time in Black Mountain Pass, the most peaceful town in his jurisdiction, not unless some crime was committed. As a result, he knew only the dregs of the town—a rowdy lot, as in most mining towns— and a few of the big shots. Everyone in Coal County knew Everett Ganner and, of course, the Prestons and Kenwells, whose faces constantly appeared in the society pages of the Durmont Daily. He knew Bernie Slade too, but not from the society page. He had arrested him a few times several years back for drunk and disorderly conduct.

As McQuede started down the rutted dirt road toward Bernard Slade's dilapidated house, he wondered what Loris' words had been meant to imply. Did she know more about the fights between father and son than she was willing to tell?

The neighborhood became more dismal the further south he headed, each dwelling, filled with noisy kids and barking dogs, more run-down than the last. Bernie Slade's house was set off by itself. McQuede swung the squad car into the yard, skimming the old frame building, the sagging roof and rotting boards. The surrounding land was dotted with rusted car bodies, scraps of iron, and piles of junk that belonged in the town dump. A barking dog sounded an alarm, and a stooped, wizened old man appeared at the doorway, squinting at McQuede as if the sun hurt his eyes. "What do you want with me? I'm clean and sober."

One look at him told McQuede he was neither. He hadn't had trouble with Bernie lately, but from the looks of him, the old man wasn't in the best of health, probably doing most of his drinking alone, sticking close to home.

"I just dropped by to ask you a few questions," he said.

"Wasting your time. Don't have any answers."

"The Coal County Museum was broken into last night."

"What would I want with that trash?" His veined hand swept with annoyance around the clutter. "Got plenty of things like that myself."

"I heard you attended the open house." When the old man didn't respond, McQuede added, "I didn't take you for a history buff."

McQuede could smell last night's whiskey on his breath.

It seemed to have permeated the wrinkled folds of his half-buttoned shirt, seeped all the way through to his skin.

"I just went for the eats. Don't cook much anymore, and they usually put out quite a spread. All for free."

"Someone stole a picture, a class photograph."

Bernie now ventured out onto the porch and sank into one of several rickety chairs. "Sure wasn't me."

"It had a picture of your son, and below his name someone had written *never graduated*." McQuede, hoping the chair would hold him, eased himself down beside Bernie. "Thought you might have taken issue with it being on display, maybe carted it off. If you did, no big problem. I'll just return the picture quietly, no hassle."

Bernie rankled, saying belligerently, "I sure didn't steal no picture! Yeah, I saw what was written there, and all I can say is, it serves him right. As far as I'm concerned, I never had a son. Or a wife either." His voice lowered, and McQuede thought he recognized a note of regret. "It was hard on me after my wife up and left. Dumped the boy on me too, but I raised him the best I could. Not that Jerome was any help. Always strumming that old guitar. Wouldn't have dreamed of getting a real job and helping me out."

The flimsy chair squeaked as McQuede shifted positions. "I heard that Jerome and a few of his friends started a band."

"That'd be Everett, Harlan, and Bruce. Harlan was a no-good scoundrel, still is. He led my boy into a lot of trouble. Bruce wasn't much better, but he straightened out, got a good job down at the school, takin' pictures, and writin', and the like. The Ganner kid hung around here a lot, too.

Ev Ganner lived just down the way, in that row of houses you passed by. Always liked that one. Talked to him a long time last night. Always knew he'd make good."

McQuede glanced toward the houses Bernie referred to, dismal places run by a slumlord who ignored leaking roofs and broken pipes. It seemed unbelievable that the high school principal had sprung from such poor roots.

The old man, in a talking mood now, said, "There was a girl too. Jerome was smitten with her. Girl named Heather. Forget her last name, but she was a real looker and could sing like a bird. I heard they planned to run off together." He gave a bitter laugh. "I told the boy she'd never leave her rich daddy for the likes of him."

"Why did Jerome leave town so quickly?"

The old man gave a snort. "Had the cops questioning him, that's why. He got into bad company, was a suspect in a string of robberies around town."

Bernie clenched his wiry, knotted hands. He was older now and in poor health, but McQuede remembered just a few years back when the man had been all pointed boots and flailing fists, how it had taken all of McQuede's strength to subdue him, to force him into the squad car.

"Yep, I was glad to see the last of that boy. I was good to him, I'll tell you that. The last time I saw him, he told me he wanted to take Heather to a school dance. I turned two of my credit cards over to him, one for gas, the other for flowers and such. You know what he did? He stole my cards, and I never saw him again."

"Did he take any of his personal things, clothes, musical instruments?"

"I'm not sure about that. Didn't need them, anyway. I

had credit then, a good job at the mine. I didn't know what had happened until I got the statements. That little sneak spent my two cards right up to the limit. Yes, sir, he knows if he ever had the nerve to come around here again, I'd run him off." The veined hands doubled into fists again, the threat seeming pathetic and empty.

McQuede left the old man with his angry memories. As he crossed to his squad car, he stopped a moment and looked back. A pretty landscape, if it hadn't been ruined by rusted car bodies and piles of debris. Thickets of sagebrush and juniper trees led down to a little creek. As his gaze roved over the land, he wondered if the old man had lied about the credit card theft to throw him off the track, knowing McQuede would not be able to trace any transactions after all this time. He wondered if Jerome Slade and his father had gotten into a violent fight, and if Jerome was buried out there somewhere, the victim of a drunken argument with his old man. Maybe the boy had never left town after all.

Chapter Three

McQuede drove slowly through the ramshackle district, thinking of ragtag boys dreaming of success. He thought of one in particular, Jerome Slade, and decided, even after all these years, to do his best to locate Bernie's son.

He called his deputy, Sid Carlisle, and explained the situation. "See if you can trace Jerome Slade though social security records. Run a criminal check too. I want to be sure he hasn't been detained these past twenty years in some prison."

"Will do. I'll get back with you as soon as I can."

McQuede drove down Main Street, past the Spence Art Gallery, the homey front of Mom and Pop's Café, and The Drifter bar. He stopped at the Black Mountain State Bank, owned for the most part by the Prestons. Likely Fredrick Preston III, who divided his time between the bank and the Preston Coal Mine, would be there now. A good place to begin would be to find out what he could from the most prominent member of the Class of '88.

McQuede headed up a winding flight of stairs toward

16

Preston's office. He lingered on the balcony for a moment, looking down at the smattering of people standing at teller windows and lobby desks. Then he walked toward the open door to Preston's office. As he approached, Preston quickly and furtively hung up his phone.

"Are you looking for me, Sheriff?" Preston asked, one thin hand remaining on the desktop. He rose as McQuede entered. "How may I help you?"

"I didn't stop by for a loan," McQuede said, smiling. "I just need some information. If you have a minute."

Preston's gaze strayed to the wall clock, but he answered politely. "Have a chair." Preston settled himself behind the desk and regarded McQuede with stern eyes, as black as his pencil-thin mustache.

"I'm looking into the disappearance of Jerome Slade," McQuede stated.

Preston raised dark eyebrows. "Why now? So many years have passed."

McQuede, not commenting, continued, "I understand you went to high school with him."

"We were never friends," Preston replied quickly, seeming to make a vague reference to the fact that Jerome came from a completely different social level. "But I'll tell you all I can. What do you want to know?"

McQuede leaned back in his chair. "To begin with, what sort of reputation did Jerome have?"

"He didn't fit in with the rest of us," Preston said, almost resentfully. "He wasn't well liked. Perhaps I should qualify that. None of the boys liked him much, but the girls swooned over him and bought into his crazy stories about becoming a rock star."

"Any girl in particular?"

Preston looked away. "I'd say they all liked him." Coldness crept into Preston's voice. "Everyone's dream boy." He rose suddenly, staring churlishly down at McQuede. "What is this all about?" he demanded. "Jerome left Black Mountain years ago. No one cared then. And no one cares now."

"I do," McQuede replied.

Preston walked to the door and stood with one hand on the knob. Aware that he was being dismissed, McQuede got to his feet. "I'm going to find him for Bernie Slade's sake."

"Bernie didn't ask you to locate him, did he?" Iciness still lurked in Preston's voice.

"Not in so many words."

"Not at all," Preston corrected. "The two of them fought like animals. The best day of the old man's life was when Jerome Slade left Black Mountain Pass for good."

"Whether Bernie wants me to or not," McQuede returned, "it's my job and I'm going to do it."

"If I were you, I wouldn't bother. Locating him is not worthwhile. He harmed everyone he ever knew. It would be like looking for a deadly rattler."

For some reason, Fredrick Preston didn't want Slade found, and to McQuede this was singularly puzzling.

McQuede left the bank and headed across the street to Mom and Pop's Café. The owner's name was Katie Jones, but most people just called her Mom. She was one of his best sources of information. She'd spent years leaning over the counter, laughing at jokes, and sharing gossip. She was comforting, as mothers are, and always the same, her graying hair pulled back from a plump, happy face.

Ev Ganner, gray suit stretching tautly across his broad shoulders, perched at the counter. Mom was chattering to him as she polished and arranged napkin holders and salt and pepper shakers. McQuede sat down beside him, saying, "What are you doing here this time of day? Shouldn't you be at the school?"

"This is my main office," Ganner replied with a hardy laugh. "And yours too, I see."

Mom quickly supplied McQuede with a steaming mug of coffee. "You look as if you could use this. Out on some big case, I suppose?"

"Might turn out to be one." McQuede curled his hands around the mug. "Do you remember Jerome Slade?"

Even though he was addressing Mom, Ganner answered, "Sure. We grew up together." He smiled and rubbed a hand across his cleft chin. "We were both raised in Black Mountain's very own shantytown, and I'm proud of it!"

"Bernie told me Jerome and you were good friends."

"As children, but before he left here, he started going one way and me another."

"You mean he started going bad?"

"I didn't hear myself saying that," Ganner replied with another pleasant smile. "We just started pursuing different interests, that's all. I started thinking about college and getting a real job, while he still thought he'd make something out of that small-time rock band."

"I remember him best as a young boy," Mom broke in. "Such a cute little fellow." She stopped what she was doing and leaned against the counter. "Sometimes I'd pay him to sweep the floor. He always tickled me. He'd stuff that money into his pocket and say real importantlike that he was going to save it." She straightened up and began wiping the counter. "Gosh, I haven't thought about Jerome for years. Hope he isn't in any trouble."

Ganner turned his full attention to finishing his home-baked cinnamon roll.

"You don't happen to know where he was headed when he left Black Mountain Pass?"

"No," Mom said. "One day he just quit coming in. When I heard he'd left town," she added, "I couldn't believe he hadn't even stopped to say goodbye to me."

"He probably struck out for California as young rebels have been doing for decades," Ganner remarked. "A lot of kids get mixed up with drugs there and die a John Doe."

"Oh, Ev, I can depend on you to think the worst. One time Jerome told me he was saving all the money he could so he could become a big star. I think that just might have happened."

"I haven't seen him on TV." Ganner rose and selected a bill from his wallet. Without glancing toward McQuede, he asked, "Why are you looking for him? Is he wanted for some crime?"

"Maybe he is a victim of one. In any event, I *do* intend to find him."

"And he will," Mom said admiringly. "When Jeff gets on someone's trail, he just never gives up!"

"How do you intend to locate someone who's been missing for over twenty years?" Ganner asked.

"First by talking to his old classmates, beginning with those who have remained in Black Mountain. I understand that another childhood pal of his—and yours—is that photographer, Bruce Fenton. He still works at the high school, doesn't he?"

"He teaches just one class at three o'clock. But if you want to locate Jerome, you should be visiting his old girlfriends: Heather Kenwell—used to be Preston, but took back her maiden name—or Loris Conner."

McQuede felt a jolt. So after all these years, Loris still held the label of Jerome's old girlfriend. Realizing Ganner was waiting for his reply, McQuede said hurriedly, "I'll start with Bruce. Leave the best for last."

McQuede pulled to a stop outside the high school and remained in the squad car. The two-story building, rocks darkened with age, probably dated back to the 1930s. It had small, old-fashioned windows, often opened wide to let in the cool, mountain air. The only modern part was the gym, a metal annex added about twenty years ago. Like the school, it too was slated for demolition.

The old building, filled with lifetimes of memories, was going to be torn down despite community protests. The elite circle who made the decisions—the Prestons and the Kenwells—were convinced that destruction represented progress.

McQuede got out slowly, his thoughts on what had happened to Jerome. As he entered the wide hallway, a feeling of uneasiness gripped him, almost as if he were being greeted by a ghost. A sixth sense had always alerted him to trouble. In this instance, the warning might still lie ahead, or might be buried in the past, but it was very much present. As he walked down the hallway toward the office, the ghost seemed to float along beside him. McQuede attempted to dispel the feeling and immerse himself in familiar noises, in the mingled voices of students and teachers.

"Where can I find Bruce Fenton?" he asked the young desk clerk.

"You're in luck. He usually doesn't come in until right before class. But he's here now, cleaning out his office, moving everything to the new school or to his shop downtown."

"Is he on this floor?"

"Number 13," she returned.

Room 13—that didn't do anything to alleviate McQuede's apprehension. He found the number at the end of the hall and rapped loudly. The low-pitched, raspy voice seemed to drift to him from some distance away. "Come on in."

McQuede opened the door, met by darkness that caused him to stop dead-still in the threshold. Then, from a far corner, a dim light came on in conjunction with the sound of a motor. The beam of an old-style projector cast creepy shadows across Bruce Fenton's face.

"I've been reviewing some of my old slides," he said. "Switch on that light, will you?" He stared at McQuede through small, round glasses, his sharp eyes seeming to cut like a laser. The brightness enhanced the deep grooves in the thin face framed by strands of long, graying brown hair, giving him the appearance of someone stuck in the past. McQuede could see why the kids called him "Freaky Fenton."

"Can't bring myself to throw anything out," he said. "Guess I'll just have to haul everything down to the studio."

The studio Fenton referred to, a small hole-in-the-wall photography shop, sat in the center of town, sunk between the *Black Mountain Herald* and Baxter's Grocery Store.

Gravelike silence settled between them, one Fenton didn't break with any inquiries. To McQuede, his own words seemed loud and forced. "I'm doing some checking on an old classmate of yours, Jerome Slade."

Fenton continued to stare at him without speaking.

"Have you seen or heard from him since he left Black Mountain Pass?"

"No, not since the Spring Fling Dance some twenty years ago."

Fenton pushed back his chair and got to his feet. The effort seemed awkward and stiff, as if he had been sitting in the same position for a very long time. Standing, he looked even thinner. The slight slope to his shoulder from years of bending over photographs added to his odd appearance.

"Mr. Ganner probably told you about the unusual theft from the museum. Are you the one who wrote that note *never graduated,* below Jerome's picture?"

"Yes. After Jerome left, I thought of deleting the photo, but I printed that below it instead. The class just didn't seem complete without him."

"When was the last time you saw Jerome?"

"Jerome left the dance at midnight. A lot of kids were still there. I hung around late as I was the school photographer. I spent the evening taking pictures." Fenton turned from him to fumble through several of the surrounding boxes. "In fact, I just ran across this one."

He showed McQuede a large black-and-white photo.

"There's Heather Kenwell and Jerome Slade dancing.

Photography was more fun before digital cameras and all that. I do my best work with black-and-white, 35-millimeter film." He ran a thin finger along the edge of the photo, as if caressing it. "Notice the way the light catches their garments."

Fenton seemed more concerned about his expert work than about why McQuede had contacted him. Or was there another reason Fenton's gaze seemed fixated on the attractive Heather Kenwell?

"See that table behind them?" Fenton asked.

McQuede recognized Fredrick Preston, looking quite the same minus the pencil-thin mustache. On one side of him were vacant chairs, on the other Loris Conner. Both of them were staring at the focal point of the shot—the pretty blond girl and her devil-may-care partner.

"Heather looked so beautiful that night," Fenton said, his voice wavering a little. "She could have had any guy she wanted. It was quite a stir when she threw over Fredrick Preston and went to the dance with Jerome."

Once again, Fenton's gaze lingered on the photograph of Heather, a strange glow lighting his eyes. Slade, Preston, and Fenton too—had all of them been in love with her?

As if realizing he had focused on Heather too long, Fenton pointed to a man in the background. "That's Heather's father, State Senator Kenwell. He and his wife attended every school function, this one as well, although they didn't approve of Heather's choice of partners. You know Senator Kenwell died last May, don't you? A heart attack."

"Yes, I heard. Who's the girl seated beside Heather's parents?"

"She was my date, Diane. I married her, and we have four kids."

McQuede wondered if his brood of four all acted as weird as he did. "You were quite a photographer, even then," McQuede said. "But at that time, if I remember right, you were thinking of going for a musical career."

"A few of us got together and formed a band called *Orion.* I've always been highly creative," he boasted. "I used to express myself through poetry. I wrote a lot of the songs for the band. But it was Jerome who made them come to life."

"Who else was in your group?"

"Everett Ganner fooled around with the guitar, but he wasn't very good at it. Harlan Daniels was a better musician. Could play anything. And ambitious too. He found us a manager that he met at The Drifter. This guy had connections, was going to set us up with shows in Vegas. But nothing ever came of it."

"Who was this would-be manager?"

"I think he's still here in town. I forgot his name. You'll have to ask Harlan. Harlan runs The Drifter now, you know."

"What was the state of the band at the time Jerome vanished?"

Those sharp, cynical eyes met McQuede's. "Ready to split up. We hung on as long as we could. We were young and dumb. Jerome always had high hopes, but the rest of us figured out at last that it was just a pipe dream. My reality turned out to be a wife and four kids to support. I'm just glad to have a steady paycheck."

"Do you have any more photos of that dance?"

"Lots of them." Fenton looked in exasperation at the clutter around him. "But where? They're lost in the shuffle. If I run across any more, I'll be glad to show them to you."

McQuede started to leave, but turned back to ask, "After the band split up, was there any chance Jerome went to Vegas on his own?"

"Not a chance." A tone of resentment crept into Fenton's voice. "You know the story of Cyrano? Jerome had stage presence and the kind of looks girls went crazy over, but I had all the talent. He couldn't have gotten along without my songs any more than Christian de Neuvillette could have wooed Roxanne without the help of Cyrano. Maybe I'm secretly glad he didn't make it big—he didn't deserve it. Why should he have gotten famous when I'm stuck here?"

Fenton turned back to his work.

McQuede left the office and wandered around the school where classes were being held for almost the last day. Display cases had been emptied, and photos that once lined the long corridor had been removed. The demolition was scheduled, and the process of closing out the building was almost concluded.

For old-time's sake, McQuede wandered toward the gym where his home team of Durmont had played against Black Mountain Pass. He stood for a while in the doorway, his thoughts lost in memories of cheering crowds and fast-hurled basketballs. The consolidation of their schools meant no more competition between the two towns.

He ambled forward between the walls that separated the bleachers on either side. As he did, a paperback book fell from above and hit the floor with a thud. He glanced up toward the second floor to the shelflike enclosure that adjoined the walls and blocked off the top entrance, now piled with boxes and equipment meant to be salvaged.

McQuede stooped to pick up the book at his feet. Just as he did, a heavy object from far above struck his shoulder. The enormous force knocked the breath from him and hurled him forward. Jabs of pain spread throughout his body. He attempted to get to his feet, but blackness overtook him, and he slumped to the floor, stunned.

Chapter Four

W hat's happened?"

Through a blurry haze, McQuede saw Bruce Fenton staring down at him. How had he gotten here so quickly?

"Are you hurt badly?" Fenton was leaning over him, his eyes bright and intense behind small, round glasses.

"I'm fine. Just give me a minute." The room spun around as McQuede struggled to his feet. He brought a hand to his aching shoulder. The impact had ripped his shirt. Even though no blood flowed, the realization that he had so narrowly escaped serious injury left him shaken.

An old-style scoreboard, surrounded by broken glass, had spun off to his left and settled a few feet from him.

"While the workers were clearing the gym," Fenton said, "they must have left this heavy sign balanced on that narrow ledge up there."

The old scoreboard could not have fallen of its own accord. Someone must have been crouched above waiting for him to enter. Moving the makeshift weapon in line with McQuede had probably caused the book to fall. McQuede stared up at the balcony. If it hadn't been for his bending to retrieve the book, he would have been hit squarely on the head, a vicious blow likely to have proven fatal.

Fenton echoed McQuede's own thoughts, saying with alarm, "You're lucky you didn't get killed."

"What was that noise?" Everett Ganner, face flushed, rushed into the gym.

"Just as the sheriff walked in," Fenton explained, "this thing fell from overhead."

Ganner stepped closer. "Let's have a doctor check you out. We've got liability. That will take care of everything."

"Don't worry, I'm not suing anyone," McQuede asserted. "No broken bones. I'm fine."

"Why would anyone stack heavy equipment on that ledge?" Ganner snapped, looking directly above them. "I'll see some heads rolls for this! Pure carelessness, that's what it is!"

"Calm down, Ev," Fenton said soothingly. "An accident, that's what it was, a simple accident."

As the two men exchanged glances, McQuede's foreboding returned full force.

Ganner spoke reluctantly. "I guess accidents do happen."

No chance this was an accident, McQuede thought. Someone had intended to stop him from investigating Jerome Slade's disappearance.

He looked from Ganner to Fenton, wondering if one of them had pushed the scoreboard off the balcony. His thoughts drifted to Fredrick Preston and to the abrupt way he had ended that phone call at the bank. Had he heard of McQuede's investigation and contacted someone with the intention of making McQuede a target?

"Let's get this cleaned up," Ganner said.

Suspecting that no fingerprints would be found on the scoreboard, but still hopeful, McQuede replied, "Let's just leave things as they are until my boys get here."

McQuede waited until his deputies had arrived, and then he went home to nurse his wounds. The pain in his shoulder had increased, and huge bruises now darkened his skin. He sank down in his recliner by the window, a cup of coffee in hand. After a while, he reached for the phone and rang his office. "Sid, Fredrick Preston made a call from the bank about ten o'clock this morning. I need to know the name of the person he contacted."

A long time passed before his deputy got back to him. "The call was made from the bank to the residence of Loris Conner."

Loris' face materialized in McQuede's mind, causing him to hesitate. "Have you had any luck tracing Jerome Slade though his social security number?"

"No."

"How about the criminal check?"

"Nothing shows up."

"Thanks." McQuede replaced the receiver and again lifted the cup, now filled with tepid coffee. His hands tightened convulsively around it. Doubts no longer existed in his mind—Jerome Slade had been murdered.

Questions raced through McQuede's mind. While at the bank, why had Preston called Loris at that particular time and hung up so covertly? Could this group of high school classmates all possess some incriminating knowledge concerning Jerome's fate, knowledge they wanted to keep concealed?

After that call from Preston, Loris might have talked to someone who had taken it upon himself to stage a near-fatal accident. Ev Ganner and Bruce Fenton had both been nearby when the scoreboard had fallen. Either one or both of them could be part of a conspiracy to cover up Jerome's murder.

McQuede didn't like to see Loris Conner frown. He always pictured her with a carefree laugh or with the smile that lit her eyes whenever she saw him. He had to remind himself as he sank into the chair across from her desk that he probably meant nothing to her, just one in a long list of men who found her attractive.

"I just heard about the accident," she said. "Ev called me. He told me it could have been a real disaster. I'm so glad you're all right."

"I came here first, because I think I can get some straight answers from you." He watched her frown deepen and tenseness form around her lips. "You talked to Preston this morning at ten. Would you mind telling me what he told you?"

She looked away from him. "Fredrick is my biggest donor. He has an idea for another benefit to raise money for the museum."

"Did he mention Jerome or my plan to investigate his disappearance?"

"No, he didn't."

McQuede studied her. He thought he was skilled at knowing when someone was lying, but with her, he wasn't sure. "I want you to think back to the last time you saw Jerome, that night of the spring dance."

"You should be talking to Heather Kenwell. She was his date that evening."

McQuede visualized the picture Bruce Fenton had shown him—the hurt way Loris was staring at the couple on the floor, the dark expression on Fredrick Preston's face as he too watched them.

Loris' words seemed edged with some old sadness. "The two of them had made plans to run off together that night."

"So close to graduation? Why?"

"You remember Heather's father, Senator Kenwell, don't you? He had an aura of power about him, a man who was never content unless he won. He was greatly opposed to his daughter seeing Jerome. He had plans of his own, for her to marry into the Preston family. Heather is every bit as headstrong as her father was, so they clashed. She decided to get her way by running off with Jerome."

"How did Fredrick Preston take that news?"

"Not well. Until Jerome showed up, it was always Fredrick and Heather. He's always been in love with her. Too bad, when they finally married, that it didn't work out."

McQuede remarked, "How well did you know Jerome?"

"Jerome was failing English, and he had to have that credit to graduate. English had always been my best subject. Mrs. Hughes asked me to tutor him, which I was doing at the time he left."

"Did he tell you he was leaving?"

She hesitated. "As I told you, secrets are often not secrets here in Black Mountain Pass."

"Did you talk to him the evening he disappeared?"

"Of course. We were seated at the same table."

"You didn't see him after the dance ended, though?"

Loris made no verbal reply, just a small shake of her head.

McQuede rose, trying to rid himself of his doubts.

"Heather is really the one you should talk to about Jerome."

McQuede glanced back at her as he left the office. Her worried image stayed with him as he headed toward the old Kenwell mansion.

Before he had reached Main Street, he noticed a black truck following him. The heavy-duty Ford, similar to those used at a coal mine or a construction site, had pulled out of a parking space near the museum just as he had left. Whoever was behind him was driving slowly now, keeping a measured distance away.

McQuede turned the corner. Soon the truck appeared in the rearview mirror, staying behind him like an ominous shadow. First the accident at the school, now some unknown person tracking his every move.

The truck had a Wyoming license plate, but the numbers were mud-spattered and unreadable. The only distinguishing feature was a slight dent near the left headlight. He could not get a good view of the driver because of the lowered sun visor.

McQuede drove slowly down the block, then unexpectedly made a quick U-turn. The truck screeched to a stop, backed up, and veered around the corner out of sight. McQuede turned on the siren and pursued him. By the time he reached the intersection, the truck had completely vanished.

McQuede searched diligently through empty alleys and quiet streets. At long last he admitted that his search was useless.

McQuede kept close watch as he headed for the mountainous area outside of town, dominated by the opulent Kenwell estate. The house sat behind a high, wrought-iron fence. With its dark, towering walls and small windows it looked aloof and secluded—a keeper of secrets.

McQuede stood immobile in front of the squad car thinking of Senator Kenwell. Being prideful and inflexible, he wouldn't have stood by while Heather ran away with a nobody. He might very well have stepped in to protect his daughter. Jerome and he could have faced off the night of the dance. That might be the source of the conspiracy, if one existed: a cover-up by those who had witnessed his actions, all of them united by a willingness to protect the town's hero from a murder charge.

News did have a way of getting around in Black Mountain Pass. Heather Kenwell met him at the door with an abruptness that made him certain she had been expecting him.

"Come in, Sheriff," she said. Her cordial manner contradicted the coldness in her eyes.

McQuede wasn't the type to have been invited to the plush Kenwell home. He'd always shied away from men like Kenwell, who used their power to sponsor themselves and their own highly profitable interests. Fact was, Kenwell had written many well-honed articles in the *Black Mountain Herald* supporting McQuede's rivals. McQuede could almost see, as he stepped into the spacious front hall, the swarms of elegant guests who had come and gone at Kenwell's bidding. But the old man was dead now, and McQuede stood looking at the woman to whom his torch had been tossed. He liked her, he decided, about as well as he had her father.

Heather's thick blond hair, every short strand smartly in place, spoke of success. So did the fashionable, dark blue pantsuit. She led him toward the fireplace, and with great self-assurance, like her charismatic father, asked, "What do you want to talk to me about?"

"Jerome Slade."

She did not react to either the name or his shortness of explanation.

"This fall I am running for the state senate," she said, the coldness in her eyes creeping into her voice. "I have one strike against me, divorcing Fredrick Preston. I don't want another one." Her words became slower, more certain. "I won't be associated in any way with what might have happened twenty years ago to Jerome Slade."

"There's lots of happenings in my life I'd like to forget too," McQuede remarked. "But facts are facts, aren't they?"

"I was very young then," Heather said. "I should have known better than to have ever been seen with him."

"More than just being seen together," McQuede replied. "I hear you were planning to leave Black Mountain with him."

"That didn't happen, did it?"

"Why not is what I'm wondering."

She never wavered, but continued staring him down. "I was a schoolgirl then, crazy about him, or the great star he convinced me he was going to become."

"Did you plan to leave from the dance that night?"

"Yes, we did."

"What did your father think about that?"

"He didn't know of our plans. But Daddy was a true democrat. He believed in everyone making his or her own decisions."

"What happened that night?"

"I went home, and then came back to the dance. We were to meet in the new auditorium that the school was building then."

McQuede's aching shoulder reminded him of just how well he knew the spot.

"I waited for hours, but Jerome didn't show up." She stopped in solemn remembrance. "That broke my heart right in two. I had always dated Fredrick Preston, and I married him on the rebound. Another mistake." The toss of her head rearranged the blond curls. "I plan now to make my own way without the interference of any man."

Since no one had seen him after that night, Jerome had likely been killed at the Spring Fling Dance. "Did you ever find out why Jerome didn't show up?" McQuede asked. "Did you hear from him after he left?"

"No. But several weeks before the dance, he started acting strange. I thought maybe he'd changed his mind about me, that he'd fallen for someone else."

McQuede thought of Loris.

"But I decided that wasn't the reason. Jerome was always reaching for the stars. I think he was deeply associated with some crooked scheme to get the money to build his dreams on. He probably had to leave here or face criminal charges."

"That could be. His father said he was mixed up with the

wrong crowd. Do you think Jerome was involved in those robberies occurring in Black Mountain at the time?"

"I think that would be a good question for Harlan Daniels," she returned. "He kept dragging Jerome down—down to his level." She straightened her tall, slender frame. "That's all I know, and I don't want to talk to you about this again."

Chapter Five

Loud laughter and music flowed from The Drifter out into the street. At night the rowdiness got worse, and the bar was the scene of many arrests. It was a favorite hangout of Frank Larsh, better known as Ruger. That was because of his choice of weapon, a .357 Ruger Blackhawk that he was known to show off when drunk—and that McQuede had been known to confiscate on numerous occasions.

Ruger was the closest to an outlaw that Black Mountain Pass had. McQuede had a feeling that his trading business, which he operated from the old, sprawling ranch he had inherited from his parents, was a front for much shadier enterprises. Rumors abounded that he had his hand in numerous crimes, including the transfer of stolen goods, artifact smuggling, and car theft—all unsubstantiated. McQuede suspected Ruger was guilty of *something,* but *what,* he had yet to discover, let alone prove.

As McQuede stepped into the dim room, the brawny, biker-type bartender boomed out, "Run, everyone. Here comes the sheriff!"

Harlan Daniels had been the tavern manager for many years. Daniels was fit and muscular except for the slight potbelly that strained his black T-shirt. He was bald on top, as if the reddish brown hair that had once covered his head had slipped down to his chin.

A few regulars lounged at tables watching a big TV. McQuede's nemesis, Ruger, swung around on the bar stool, cowboy hat pulled rakishly low over shocks of sand-colored hair. He gave McQuede a big smile. "Buy you a drink, Sheriff?"

"I'm on duty," McQuede replied, imagining Ruger would fall off his bar stool if he one day took him up on the offer. Ruger always baited him, going just far enough.

"If you don't want a drink, what do you want?" Daniels asked, nervously placing aside a bottle on the bar. McQuede's presence seemed to make him uneasy, as if he were thinking of all the minor laws habitually broken at The Drifter.

"No new trouble," McQuede replied. "I'm just checking up on an old story."

Harlan lifted the bottle again, poured a glass, and slid it toward Ruger. McQuede could imagine a younger version of the big, balding bartender as part of a band, those tattooed and muscular forearms banging on a set of drums.

"You heard from Jerome Slade lately? I understand the two of you were buddies. I'm trying to locate him."

Out of the corner of his eye, McQuede watched Ruger lean forward so he wouldn't miss any of their conversation. It annoyed him the way Ruger made everything his business.

"No, we lost touch," Harlan said, "a long time ago."

"I heard that a group of you had started a band."

"That was more than twenty years back. The band was breaking up even then. And you can see for yourself what became of my musical plans."

"You were trying to save your career, though, weren't you? Someone told me you had lined up a manager for the band."

Harlan glanced warily from McQuede to Ruger.

"That'd be me," Ruger suddenly broke in, a grin spreading across his face.

"You?" McQuede echoed in surprise. He should have known Ruger would have a hand in this somewhere. "I didn't know you were managing rock bands."

"That was in my ribald youth," Ruger said smoothly. "I've since retired from the music business." Ruger was in his mid-forties, but mug shots of him in his early twenties looked much the same; like the story of the *Portrait of Dorian Gray,* he never seemed to age. He still gave the illusion of youth, except for his eyes, now cold as stone.

"Maybe I should be talking to you then. Did you steer Jerome toward some promising job?"

"As I recall, the boy came to me to see if I could set his fledgling band up with a gig or two. Had a kind of dreamy name to it. Stardust? Zephyr?"

"Orion," Harlan supplied, as if the band's identity was still important to him, even after all these years.

"I put him in contact with my Vegas connection, a friend of mine who you know well, Sammy Ratone."

Sammy made frequent trips to Black Mountain Pass to see Ruger, no doubt on some shady business. Sammy,

Ruger's partner in crime, was his exact opposite, a city
crook with slicked-back black hair and shiny loafers. But
despite outward appearances, they were two of a kind.

"So you acted as middleman."

"I set up the appointment with Sammy, and he agreed to
talk to the kid. If the band was any good, Sammy was going
to set them up with a gig or two. I was supposed to get a
kickback," Ruger explained, "a manager's cut."

"I don't think Jerome ever followed through," Harlan
broke in.

McQuede turned back to Ruger. "Did Jerome Slade ever
go to Vegas and book with Sammy?"

Ruger shrugged. "All I know is that I never saw a dime."

"Is this McQuede?" The phone call was interrupted by
a racking cough, then a raw, wheezy voice announced,
"Bernie Slade. Can you drop by? I've found something that
may be important."

A short time later McQuede sat at a rickety kitchen table
where Bernie had proudly spread the contents of an old cigar box. "My wife always nagged me about being a pack-
rat. She said, 'Bernie, you never throw nothin' away.' Guess
she was right." With a sweep of his hand, he gestured toward a bundle of yellowed papers neatly bound with a rub-
ber band.

As McQuede lifted the stack of what turned out to be
credit card statements, he felt Bernie Slade's small, bright
eyes eagerly watching him.

"Will this help?"

Back before debit cards, each credit card transaction
was imprinted by a special machine, which made several

duplicate copies. One remained with the merchant and a carbon copy was given to the customer as a receipt. When Jerome charged anything, he probably stuffed the receipts in his wallet or pocket, but the monthly credit card statement, including an itemized account of each individual transaction, had been sent back to Bernie.

The transactions, with the first ones dated the Monday after the school dance, made a clear paper trail of gas stations, restaurants, and motels through Wyoming, Utah, and Nevada. Curiously, the last transaction was from a casino in Las Vegas, Sammy's Place, owned by Sammy Ratone. Jerome, still underage, must have used a false ID, which made his movements that much harder to trace.

Bernie looked at McQuede, suddenly hopeful. "Think this'll help find him?"

McQuede realized the old man really did care. "So now you want him found?"

Bernie shrugged. "Blood's thicker than water. He's the only kin I've got left. I'd kind of like to know what became of him."

"Mind if I take these statements with me? I'll make copies and return them."

"That's what I dug them out for. If you find my boy . . ."

"You'll be the first to know," McQuede promised.

McQuede had found his first real lead. The credit card statements indicated that Jerome Slade had left Black Mountain Pass alive and had made a trip to Vegas. McQuede's next order of business would be to find out whether or not Jerome had met with Sammy Ratone. If he could persuade Sammy to break long-established patterns and tell him the truth, McQuede would be that much closer to finding out what had happened to the boy.

The lights of Vegas arose like a desert mirage, a magician's trick that the flick of a wand might make disappear. At the airport McQuede rented a car and drove into the city.

McQuede found himself, as usual, put off by its falseness, the lights glittering like gold to advertise gambling, a fool's game. He often wondered what people in the future, digging in the ruins, would make of it. They would probably think it had been a great temple city like the Mayan ruins, a place of worship—too bad the god here was easy money.

Vegas had changed since McQuede's last trip. The streets were much more congested on the Vegas strip than he remembered. The Four Queens and the Golden Nugget, which used to be the main attractions, now seemed overshadowed by the monolithic new casinos that had sprung up all around, eclipsing the older part of town.

McQuede drove past Circus-Circus, and then by the Paris with its high Eiffel Tower, and on past the glitzy Luxor. On one of the side streets nearing the edge of Vegas, he located Sammy Ratone's place, run-down and shabby in comparison. The neon lights winked, flashing *Sammy's Place*, *Try Your Luck*, *Can't Lose Slots*.

The clientele, even shabbier, hovered around tables or sat hypnotized by noisy slot machines. No one but the security guard bothered to look at him.

The guard drew close, saying out of the corner of his mouth, like some mafia man, "Who're you looking for, Officer?"

"Sammy Ratone," McQuede replied.

"I'll see if he's in."

The guard came back after a while and escorted him upstairs.

McQuede entered a cluttered office where Sammy sat behind a huge desk. A large name tag read Sammy Ratone. Sammy Rat would have suited him better.

Vegas may have changed, but Sammy Ratone definitely belonged to another era. He looked like some old-time, underworld gangster complete with small, deep-set eyes, crooked nose, and heavy jowls. Smoke from a not-so-expensive cigar billowed around him.

"This is my turf, McQuede," Sammy said with a big smile. "But you're welcome, I guess." He eased his short, squat form from the desk chair and extended his chubby hand.

"It's important or I wouldn't have traveled this far. I'm trying to locate a young musician who vanished from Black Mountain Pass: Jerome Slade. Last seen in the spring of 1988. Do you remember him?"

Sammy had an annoying habit of bursting out, "Ha," which he did now. "Ha! You're kidding me, aren't you? I can hardly remember what happened yesterday."

"Back then, your pal Ruger asked you to book Slade for a show or two."

Sammy, with a short, insincere laugh, sank back down. Sidestepping the question, he said, "Don't you have enough to keep you busy without digging up old cases? Or did you just want an all-paid vacation? In my opinion, you came to the wrong place. Vegas isn't what it used to be. The slots alone aren't enough anymore. Have to turn everything into an amusement park. Who'd have ever thought the big guys would try to squeeze us out? We used to *be* the big guys."

"Things change," McQuede said. Not in Ratone's case, however. He had never been anything but a two-bit crook. "But one thing hasn't changed. Jerome Slade's missing, and I want to know what happened to him."

Sammy tapped his temple. "Your problem is you think too much. Ha! But maybe not too well. Why are you so sure something happened to him? I don't recall reading his obituary."

"Jerome came to Vegas hoping to become a star. He was just a green kid with a big dream."

"So," Sammy said. "Young or old, everyone has a dream they want to cash in on. Trouble is, if you want to make it big in Vegas, you capitalize on other people's dreams."

"Is that what you did?" McQuede said. "Helped him lighten his wallet?"

Sammy grinned. "You misjudge me. I never saw the kid. But if he was as green as you say he is, I would have told him to go back home."

"So you're telling me he never even arrived at your casino?"

"That's what I'm saying."

"How do you know that? I thought you couldn't remember."

"It just came back to me. I booked him, and he was a no-show. That's all I know about him."

McQuede could usually tell when Sammy was lying. He watched to see if his squint lines would deepen, or if his eyes, easy to read without the benefit of the dark sunglasses he usually wore, would shift. No such telltale signs occurred.

McQuede persisted, "I have proof he came to Vegas."

"But do you have any proof that he talked to me?" Sammy lifted his cigar from the ashtray and took a puff, regarding McQuede smugly. "Didn't think so."

McQuede showed him the credit card statement. "How do you explain this? Not even old enough to legally gamble, and yet he managed to max out one of his father's credit cards right here in your casino."

Sammy gave the paper a quick look, then waved it away. "The statement says Bernie Slade."

"Bernie's never been to Las Vegas."

"Then someone *of age* must have stolen his wallet."

"Bernie loaned the credit cards to his son the night he disappeared. This matter concerns a human life," McQuede said brusquely. "I would think you would want to help me find Jerome."

"I would if I could," Sammy sing-songed.

McQuede turned to leave. "I'm sure of that."

"Your boy might still be in Vegas," Sammy said. "If he got into some trouble, he might have changed identities. It's easy to get lost out here."

McQuede thought about how badly Jerome wanted fast money to jump-start his career. With a phony ID, he might have tried his luck at gambling and ended up even more in debt. On the other hand, he could have gotten involved with some dangerous Vegas gangsters. McQuede gave Sammy a hard, assessing stare. "Or maybe he double-dealt someone," he said, "and ended up dead."

Sammy pulled himself to his feet and with a slow,

heavy gait followed McQuede to the door. "Now that you're here, my friend, why don't you kick up your heels a little?" He slapped a pudgy hand on McQuede's sore shoulder. "Stick around, have some fun, play the slots." Sammy thrust some papers he'd taken from his jacket pocket into McQuede's hand—coupons good for two free rolls of chips, a two-for-one exchange on twenty dollars.

McQuede tossed them into the trash can on the way out.

On the flight home, McQuede leaned back in his seat and watched the lights of Vegas disappear. Las Vegas was out of his jurisdiction, but he would report Jerome Slade as a missing person to the Nevada police and see what they could find out.

Sammy was trying to lead him to believe that Jerome was still alive, but somehow he didn't buy it. The staged accident at the school and the truck that had been tracking him had not been his imagination.

One fact was clear: someone was trying to prevent him from finding out what had happened to Jerome. McQuede had once believed Jerome had been killed at the Spring Fling Dance, but now he wondered if Jerome's last stop hadn't been at Sammy Ratone's casino.

Chapter Six

I'll have to tell Jeff about the raffle," Loris was saying. "I'm sure he'll want to buy a ticket."

McQuede, surprised to hear his name spoken, paused at the museum entranceway where Ev Ganner and Loris were standing in front of a huge poster.

Ev's booming laugh seemed to go right through him. "McQuede? His idea of art is one of those prints of dogs playing poker."

"If so, then he must be a gambling man," Loris said lightly. "Who would turn down a chance at winning the grand prize, five hundred dollars? Besides, it goes to a good cause, toward the acquisition of a Carlo Owatah painting for the museum."

"Then put me down for a few tickets." Ganner laughed. "I'll bet you're not going to get any money out of the sheriff."

"Ev, you're wrong about Jeff. Lately he's taken a real interest in art and culture. You should see how much time he spends at the museum." When Loris noticed McQuede

48

approaching, her eyes brightened. "See, here he comes now."

"Speak of the devil!"

"Jeff, would you like to buy a raffle ticket for a worthy cause? It's only five dollars."

McQuede drew out his wallet. "No sacrifice is too great for art."

"I knew I could count on you."

After collecting the money from both men, Loris bustled away, leaving McQuede alone with Ev Ganner.

McQuede studied the poster of the painting that was to be purchased with the raffle proceeds. Everyone had heard of the local part Shoshone, part Spanish painter who had risen to nationwide fame, Carlo Owatah. His most famous painting, *Ghost Warriors,* hung in the state gallery.

"Loris has wanted to acquire an original Carlo for the museum for a long time," Ganner said. "They consider him a modern-day Picasso."

The painting the museum hoped to purchase was called *Stampede*. It didn't look like much to McQuede, but he didn't say so to Ganner. Whirling parts of buffalo—eyes, ears, hooves—blended together to give the illusion of a vortex of motion. He would have liked it better if the buffalo had all been in one piece, not with their eyes over here and their mouths over there and their ears where their tails ought to be.

McQuede turned to find Ganner studying him out of the corner of his eye. "If I didn't know better, I'd think Loris was sweet on you."

"We're just friends," McQuede replied shortly.

"Just as well. I had a big crush on her back in high

school. Tried to date her, but even back then she was a regular Ice Maiden. Only had eyes for Jerome Slade. Sometimes I think she never got over him."

"I didn't know she was that close to Jerome. I thought he was involved with Heather Kenwell."

"No law says you can't love someone who doesn't love you. His taking off without a word really hurt her. Still carrying a torch—I wouldn't be surprised if that's why she's remained single all these years. She confided to me about how she's been hiding a secret pain. Jerome's disappearance left a mark on all of us." Ganner sighed deeply. "So many people live in the past. You can't dwell on yesterday. We all make bad choices, have regrets. Sometimes you just have to bury your mistakes and move on."

McQuede made no reply.

"I'm glad you're not serious about Loris. Now that I'm a widower and free myself," Ev said with a wink, "I'm hoping she'll change her mind about me."

McQuede watched him walk away. He pretended not to care, but Ganner's words stung. He thought of the old print of *A Friend in Need* that hung on the wall of his office. Maybe he didn't know much about art, but the sight of the bulldog slipping an ace to his companion always made him smile.

A weary sadness crept over him. Loris needed a man like Ganner, someone educated and cultured, who would be an asset at any social gathering and who knew a Gauguin from a Van Gogh. McQuede was way out of this league.

The weariness stayed with McQuede hours later as he drove the short distance from Black Mountain Pass to his office in Durmont. Once there, he waited for the 4:00 train to make its slow passage through the center of town, tying up traffic. The only time Durmont had a traffic jam was when the train came rattling through, blocking the entire street.

"Anything new?" McQuede asked his deputy, Sid Carlisle. Sid looked like everyone's idea of a perfect law officer: tall and slender, gray hair combed away from a lean, sharp-featured face. Efficient, as always, clutching papers, Sid trailed McQuede into his office.

"Nothing that matters much. Old Ted Baxter came in raging about that traffic light that was replaced by the four-way stop sign on East 4th. He says it caused his accident near the post office. Claims he's going to sue the city."

McQuede laughed. "I knew taking out that light was a big mistake. We'll turn that complaint over to the mayor."

"Oh, and the handyman, Wiley Clegg, he's none too happy. He reported that someone has been sabotaging his advertising. They changed the flyers he's put up all over town from 'jack-of-all-trades' to 'jackass-of-all-trades.'"

McQuede chuckled. "Same difference. But I happen to know who the culprit is. Wiley and that new repairman, Danny Richards, have been feuding ever since he moved into town. Can you find Danny and have a word with him?"

Once Sid left, McQuede moved toward the office chair behind his desk. The poker-playing dogs in the background appeared larger, covering the entire wall. For a while, after his workday was officially over, he concentrated on the growing stack of paperwork, but his thoughts kept wandering. He lifted the paperweight from his desk, watching the sunset colors of the shifting sand as he turned it in his hand.

It had been a gift from Lieutenant Alevo, a Navajo policeman from New Mexico. McQuede had helped him on a difficult case concerning a serial killer that had crossed state lines and had ended up in Wyoming.

The ever-changing patterns of the grains of sand calmed him. The blend of shifting shapes and colors reminded him suddenly of the Carlo Owatah painting, and that, in turn, reminded him of Loris.

Today, Ev Ganner had staked his claim and made clear his intentions. McQuede had to make a choice. He could either let Ganner steal Loris away, or he could compete. He lifted the phone, and before he could change his mind, punched in Loris' number.

He waited as the phone rang into emptiness. No one home. Friday night. Ganner had probably already beat him to the draw.

The mongrel dog McQuede had adopted not long ago scampered forward, jumping crazily and barking. McQuede had tagged him Psy, short for Psychotic, and the big yellow cur definitely lived up to his name. McQuede was glad that the mutt, at least, was happy to see him.

At first Psy had been wary and distrustful, now he took McQuede and the notion of being fed every night for granted. He waited patiently as McQuede poured his nightly ration into the bowl, then lost no time gulping down the food.

Good old dependable Jeffery McQuede—wasn't that

how everyone, even the dog, saw him? No doubt Loris thought of him in that way too. A confirmed bachelor, someone to bring her troubles to, not a lover, but a dependable friend.

He was only in his forties. He still had years and years ahead of him. He wasn't so sure he wanted to spend them alone. The dog finished his chow and lumbered forward, settling down beside him. McQuede smoothed the rough fur on his neck. Much as he was fond of Psy, McQuede certainly didn't want to die with his only companion a dog, one even more stubborn and overweight than he was.

On Saturday afternoon, his day off, in an attempt at self-improvement, McQuede made a trip to the library. Contrary to many people's opinion, he did like to read. He considered books good companions on long evenings. Fictional people didn't change roles or personalities. He could like them, presented as they were in their Sunday dress, without the problems that go along with actually knowing them.

He scanned the shelves of biographies and slick, mainstream novels where no one was a hero until he located the section he wanted. He didn't have time to read much, but when he did, he liked a Western, an old-fashioned shoot-'em-up, where the good guys always won. Satisfied, he pulled a Zane Gray title from the shelf.

Loris Conner reached the check-out desk about the same time as he did. She looked surprised to see him there. McQuede noticed the stack of books she was checking out, including *The Kite Runner* and other titles he had seen posted on the local book club notices.

As he slid *Shadow on the Trail* over to be checked out,

her eyes lit. "It's been a long time since I've read a Zane Gray," she said.

"Somehow, I didn't take you for a Western fan."

"My dad loved Zane Gray's writings," she replied, "and when I was a kid, I'd read anything I found in the house."

He waited for her to check out her books, and they walked out together. He hesitated only a moment, before taking the opportunity he'd been long awaiting. "I was thinking about trying out that new steakhouse tonight. If you haven't made plans for dinner, why don't you join me?"

He was surprised by her flush and by her quick reply. "I'd be glad to."

Dinner by candlelight with Loris Conner—what he had imagined for so long had become a reality. McQuede dressed carefully in a dark blue suit, fancying that it made him look taller and thinner. Loris too wore blue: a flowing skirt and silk blouse with the sheen of a summer sky.

As they waited for their meal, McQuede told her about the fight between Wiley Clegg and the poster vandal.

Loris, with a carefree laugh, said, "I have a solution. Tell Wiley to take a marking pen and beside the word 'jackass' write 'am not.' "

Their laughter broke through any reservations he'd had about the evening. Their easy conversation soon became personal.

McQuede thought about what Ganner had said concerning her carrying a torch all these years for Jerome Slade. This prompted him to ask, "I keep wondering why you've never married."

"You first," Loris said.

"I came close once. Everyone assumed Doris and I were a sure couple. But the job got in the way. Not every woman can put up with my long hours."

"I have the same reason, I guess," Loris replied. "Too busy, too many interests. Maybe I'm a little too independent. I like my space, a little alone time."

Contrary to what Ganner believed, Loris sounded like a modern woman, not someone pining away over a love lost twenty years or so ago. The thought made him happy. McQuede couldn't help noticing how beautiful she looked in the flickering light from the candles.

At first Loris was smiling, but then her gaze strayed from his, and she frowned.

He glanced over his shoulder to see Heather Kenwell leave her entourage of fans and walk toward them.

"Here comes our candidate for senator," McQuede said lightly. "Out to get our votes."

"She's the last person I want to see," Loris said in an undertone.

"I take it you don't like her very much."

"No, it's Heather who doesn't like me."

"Hi, Lor," Heather said in a condescending manner. Then she addressed McQuede, "I see you've taken to questioning suspects at expensive restaurants."

"I'm not a suspect," Loris returned, "any more than you are."

"Actually, this is my day off," McQuede drawled, attempting to prevent a clash between them.

"Don't tell me you got Lor to go on a date!" Heather commented, arching a thin, penciled brow.

Loris, as if biting back some sharp retort, glanced quickly away.

"Will this evening ever end? After this is over here, we're headed out to the Country Club for a fundraiser." Heather gestured with a toss of her head toward the waiting group, the sudden movement causing her short, blond curls to catch the overhead light. "Campaigning can be so dreary," she said, then added in a lower tone, "Look at them, will you? Big money, big heads—they're enough to ruin my dinner." She gave a rippling laugh, as if her comment was immensely clever. She started away, then turned back, calling cheerfully, "Don't forget to vote for me."

From Heather Kenwell's table in the center of the room, her high-pitched laughter and pretentious chitchat floated to them. Loris' mood had changed. This animosity stemming from high school spoiled the romantic evening McQuede had planned. Loris and he finished their final cup of coffee and left.

McQuede parked in front of Loris' house. He walked with her through a lawn scented with flowers to the door and waited as she unlocked it.

Loris turned back to him, saying, "I had a wonderful time tonight, Jeff."

He wanted to take her into his arms, but he didn't. He couldn't risk ruining what was just beginning for them. "How about another dinner, say Wednesday?"

She hesitated. "I have several meetings scheduled. I'll have to call you. Is that all right?"

Disappointed, McQuede forced himself to say "Sure."

At that moment, Loris reached for his hand. On impulse, McQuede drew her toward him. She clung to him as their lips met—not the chaste kiss between friends, but the passionate kiss of lovers.

Chapter Seven

Wednesday passed and still Loris hadn't phoned. McQuede wanted desperately to contact her, but thought it best to wait for her call. And that was going to prove difficult, for he found it impossible to blot her from his mind.

The phone on his desk rang. Hopeful, he answered it.

A very cold and businesslike voice said, "Heather Kenwell. I want to talk to you." None of the false charm she had displayed at the restaurant remained. No polite inquiry as to whether or not he was available, just the straightforward order of a person accustomed to getting her way. "Stop by Kenwell Acres this afternoon, preferably within the hour."

"I was just leaving my office. I can swing by that way now."

No goodbye, just the click of the receiver.

Heather had explicitly told him not to talk to her about Jerome again, but maybe she had changed her mind. He drove to the edge of town anxiously, hoping this would turn out to be some important lead.

Heather was waiting for him at the door. She wore a tan pantsuit that, with the high heels, made her look all legs, the image of a sophisticated model. She didn't speak until McQuede had seated himself on the couch. Then she turned to him and said adamantly, "You've got to stop him!"

"Stop who," McQuede drawled, "from doing what?"

Heather, apparently angered by his light response, glared at him. "Bruce Fenton," she snapped.

"What's he been doing?"

"That stupid camera of his is always right in my face."

"That's not against the law," McQuede reminded her. "Besides, you're big news now, running for senator. Fenton's a photographer. That's what he does, take pictures."

"He's a creep," she returned. "He's been stalking me, just as he did in high school, just as he's done all my life. As of late, he's everywhere I am."

"Have you asked him not to take any more pictures of you?"

"Yes. I did that just last night. He was hanging around the auditorium where I was speaking." She drew in a deep breath. "Every time I turn around, it's *snap, snap*. I don't have to put up with that, do I?"

"Fenton might be thinking he's helping your campaign," McQuede told her. "At any rate, he's not doing you any harm. You don't have enough grounds for a restraining order."

His calm words only flared her resolve. "You'd better take care of this for me, before it's too late. He's crazy! No telling what he'll do. Last night I looked out the window, and he was out here on my property."

McQuede rose. "I'll have a talk with him." Once at the

door, he asked, "By the way, do you know who owns a heavy-duty Ford truck, an old model?"

"Fredrick on occasion uses one of the trucks from Preston Coal. Some of them are old and all of them are black. Why do you ask?"

"Because a person in a black truck has been trailing me."

Her laugh had a hard, brittle ring. "So you have a stalker too? Well, he's not Fredrick. I think we have the same one—Freaky Fenton!"

McQuede smiled. "He may be carrying a torch for you, but I'm sure he's not for me."

McQuede studied her in silence. "Do you mind if I ask you a personal question? Do you and Fredrick have what they call a 'friendly' divorce?"

Heather waved a heavily jeweled hand. "Nothing about our relationship even approaches friendly. If we ever thought anything of one another, that was over long before we signed the divorce papers. I should have known better than to have married someone so vain and self-centered."

"I take it things went wrong for you two right from the start."

"From day one. Fredrick doesn't care about what other people want, just what he wants."

Like pairing two predators, McQuede thought.

"When we were still in high school, Fredrick had his heart set on buying a cherry red Datsun. I still remember what he called it, 'a beauty, a 300Z.' He couldn't even talk about anything else. His grandfather, that almighty Fredrick the First, gave him sixty thousand dollars for an early graduation present."

"Did he purchase the car?"

Heather tilted her head, as if it had just occurred to her that he hadn't. "No. He dropped that idea for another obsession: making me his wife. We got married right after graduation."

"Too young," McQuede remarked, and then continued, supplying a generous explanation that he knew didn't fit. "That's probably why it didn't work out."

"It didn't work out because of him. I swear, after we married, Fredrick turned into a regular penny pincher. With all that fortune behind him, with that sixty thousand in cash, you wouldn't think we'd fight constantly about money. Would you believe, I had to keep on getting an allowance from Daddy?"

McQuede rose and headed for the door, where he stopped. "Offhand, I'd say Fredrick's still in love with you."

"Offhand, I'd say that's too bad for him."

McQuede headed toward Bruce Fenton's shop, a small building wedged in between the *Black Mountain Herald* and Baxter's Grocery Store. No photographs were displayed in the small windows. He tried the knob on the glass-paneled door with the lettering *Fenton's Studio,* and found it locked.

"You're not going to find him there," Ruger called from where he stood near The Drifter. "He left early this morning loaded down with cameras. Off to take pictures of them tearing down the old high school."

McQuede set off in his squad car in this new direction and pulled in near the site. The grim process of demolition had all but been accomplished. All that remained was a wall or two and giant stacks of fallen rubble.

Apparently Fenton had come and gone. McQuede got out and leaned against the car, immersed in the clamor around him: the scrape of heavy equipment and the shouts of the work crew. Solemnly he watched the construction company owner, gray-haired Howard Birk, operating his bulldozer. The machine's huge scoop head lifted rubble from the ruins of the gymnasium and dumped it into huge bins. A sense of sadness stole over McQuede, as if he were standing in a graveyard. Soon the ground would be level, as if the building and all the pomp and circumstance of the past had never been.

"I figured you'd show up here, McQuede. You're just as sentimental as I am."

McQuede hadn't seen Ev Ganner walk up behind him. When he turned, he immediately identified with Ganner's gloom, heightened by the way his large form hunched against the cold.

"I tried everything to save the old building," Ganner lamented, like a doctor mourning a dead patient. "The only one at those meetings who backed me up was good old Fredrick, but even with his support, you see the results. It's a shame, isn't it?" The doctor simile carried over into his next words. "Lots of life was left in the old girl."

McQuede was about to reply, but deferred to the crunch of steel against rock.

"You just missed Bruce Fenton," Ganner said. "He was out here to take the last pictures of the school. Everything changes," he continued wryly, "but we'll always have Bruce's photos."

"Yes," McQuede replied without looking at him. "Fenton has a passion for preserving the past. It's fortunate that someone does."

Howard Birk, looking heavier in his coveralls, was quickly heading toward them. He looked pale and shaken. By the time he reached them, he had to stop and draw in his breath.

"Sheriff! It's a good thing you're here. We've got a big problem!"

"What?" McQuede demanded, yet his sinking heart informed him that he already had the answer.

"My boys were working right over there when I noticed some strange-looking object. I got out and saw it was a human skull." He went on, aghast. "Someone was cemented under the floor of that gym."

Ganner's skin had lost its ruddy hue. "I don't believe it."

McQuede and Ganner trailed after Burke through upheavals of stone toward the north edge of the toppled structure.

A small crowd of workers stood staring down at what had been unearthed. The skull had been pulled loose and lay atop a pile of broken cement.

McQuede traced the trail of the bulldozer back a few feet, then dropped to his knees and began carefully removing dirt. At last he found a skeleton. The bones weren't scattered, but still intact. In places, scraps of dark cloth still clung to the remains.

On one of the skeleton's fingers, McQuede found a badly tarnished and pitted silver ring. He carefully pulled it loose and studied an unusual design that looked like a pattern of stars.

Ganner knelt beside him.

"Do you recognize this?" McQuede asked.

"It looks like the ring Jerome used to wear. Those three stars done in bas relief represent the band, Orion."

McQuede thought of the constellation Orion. From what he could recall of Greek mythology, Orion had been blinded by the love of a woman.

Ganner stared down at the skeleton. Suddenly he stood up and stepped back, brushing at his jacket as if he was attempting to rid himself of dust and dirt instead of the image.

McQuede rose also and returned to the skull. He examined the damage that, at first, he thought was caused by the machine's blade. Now he realized he was looking at an old injury. The area near the temple was shattered; the victim had suffered fatal trauma to the head that had resulted in instant death. McQuede called his deputy, Sid Carlisle. "Notify the coroner's office, and then get out to the old Black Mountain high school site as soon as you can. We've got a murder."

Although no definite identification had been made, McQuede thought it best to talk to Bernie Slade and prepare him for the worst. He didn't want him to read about this discovery in the *Black Mountain Herald.*

McQuede took a deep breath before approaching the shack where Jerome's father lived. Inside, he could hear the old man shuffling around. He knocked and waited some time before the door opened a crack and a hoarse voice asked, "Who's there?"

"You got a minute?"

"I've got nothing but minutes, as you can see." Bernie stepped aside, squinting at him curiously.

McQuede walked deeper into the clutter of the room. The hodgepodge of items that surrounded him hadn't been replaced for many years: the marred table spread with beer cartons and packages of junk food, the sagging couch, the old jackets and sweaters that hung from a dilapidated hall tree. He wondered if some of those clothes had been worn by Bernie's son.

"You found out anything?" the old man rasped.

McQuede turned to him solemnly. "You know the old high school is being demolished. A body was discovered beneath the floor in the gym." He wanted to go on, but could think of nothing consoling to say. At last he added, "I thought you should know."

Bernie straightened his small frame. None of the emotion McQuede had expected appeared on his lined face, not sorrow or resignation—just a placid, stoic acceptance. "So he's dead."

"We have no positive identification yet."

"It probably couldn't be anyone else," Bernie said resignedly. "My boy hasn't been seen since the night of the dance." He looked hopefully at McQuede. "But what about those credit cards of mine that he ran up? Doesn't that mean he's still alive? Isn't that possible? Maybe someone else is buried there."

"It could happen, but I'm afraid it's unlikely."

"Who maxed out my credit cards, then?"

"If this does turn out to be Jerome, that doesn't mean he was killed the night of the dance. He might have gone to Vegas and returned."

"For Heather Kenwell!" Bennie exclaimed. "I told him not to get mixed up with high-flyin' people like the Kenwells. They'd only stomp on him, beat him down. Do you think he'd listen? No, he never heard anything I ever said, not once."

Bernie fell silent a moment, then exploded, "Old man Kenwell hated him! I'll bet he killed him!"

"We can't jump to conclusions."

"You can be sure the Kenwells are to blame. Heather Kenwell done him in, one way or another."

McQuede had one more person to tell. He drove directly to the museum, where he found Loris in her office. She rose from her desk, her face pale. "I've heard."

Loris took an uncertain step or two forward. "All these years . . . I thought—I thought Jerome was happy. I believed he was out there somewhere searching for his dream."

She stopped, tears brimming in her eyes. McQuede reached out in sympathy. His arms encircled her, and she clung to him. He smothered her hair while she cried against his shoulder.

McQuede didn't like feeling jealous of a dead man, but he couldn't help it. The signals were all too clear. Ganner had been right. The heart that McQuede wanted so desperately to win still belonged to Jerome Slade.

Chapter Eight

By late afternoon McQuede had a report back from the coroner. An examination of the skeletal remains proved what McQuede already knew. Based on old dental records and X-rays, the dead man had been positively identified as Jerome Slade.

So now McQuede was faced with a problem: how could a dead man max out credit cards? Jerome had last been seen the night of the dance, but that didn't necessarily mean that was when he had been murdered. He needed to establish a time of death, and there might be one way to find out.

As he left the office, he stopped by Sid's desk. "See if you can find out when the cement was poured at the high school gym. I'm going to talk to the major suspects and see what I can find out."

Fredrick Preston was first on his list, as he had planned to marry Heather Kenwell, who was going to throw him over for Jerome. In the squad car he called Preston.

"I'd like a word or two with you this evening."

"Can't it wait until tomorrow at the bank?"

"Now would be better."

"I'm on my way to the Country Club," Preston said, annoyed. "I'll meet you there."

McQuede headed east six miles beyond the city limits, out toward the Indian reservation, to the Country Club. He didn't belong to this set and couldn't even recall ever going inside the modern, sprawling lodge.

He recognized a few faces from the local papers sitting in front of the bar. Preston was seated at a table beside a huge window that supplied a distant view of Black Mountain, a dark, jagged image rising into the waning light of the sky. He looked up grudgingly from his drink and, in the same snappy way that Heather often spoke, said, "I hope this doesn't take long. I've got a dinner appointment."

"The body that was found at the high school was identified as Jerome Slade."

Preston said sullenly, "And that brought you to see me?"

"I want you to account for your whereabouts the night of the dance."

"I left early, about eleven o'clock. I went over to my grandfather's." Preston lifted his glass with long, thin fingers and just held it, not taking a drink. A photo-shoot pose, a Preston pose, complete with expensively cut, dark hair and a pencil-thin mustache. "I told him about Heather and me breaking up. He knew how upset I was, and he stayed up with me the rest of the night. We watched one old movie after another."

Not much of an alibi, McQuede thought, being it was from a doting grandfather. But with Mr. Preston's reputation, it would be certain to hold up in court. No one in

Black Mountain Pass was more known for telling the truth or more respected than Fredrick Preston I.

Preston set down the glass. "Now, is that all?"

"You drive one of the trucks from Preston Coal once in a while, don't you?" McQuede asked. "Have you used one recently?"

"No. I just purchased a new silver Cadillac, which is all the transportation I need."

"Do you know anyone who drives a truck like those?"

"Practically all the ranchers. Birk's Construction has one that Birk uses as a 'gofer' vehicle, and he usually parks it at all the sites. I remember seeing it near the old high school." Preston glanced at his watch. "If you've anything else to ask me, please be quick about it."

McQuede leaned back in the plush armchair and stared at him. "I understand your grandfather gave you a lot of money for your graduation present."

"He *has* a lot of money. But is that really any of your business?"

McQuede decided to push him a little further. "I just keep wondering what you did with it."

"If you ever had a wife like Heather Kenwell, you wouldn't bother to ask."

"I'm asking."

Preston shuffled uneasily in his chair. He appeared to be debating whether or not to give a direct answer.

Without a word, McQuede waited.

At last, as if on impulse, Preston said, "If you must know, I invested all the money Grandfather gave me in Billy Osterman's packing plant, and everyone who did that lost their shirts. Osterman took my money in May of '88 and a few months later, he declared bankruptcy. There went my money, all of it."

"I've listened to a lot of complaints about Osterman. Last I heard, he was in Lincoln, Nebraska."

Preston pushed his glass toward the center of the table and rose. "I can't talk to you anymore. I'll be late for the dinner."

He's concealing something, McQuede thought, as he watched him walk away. Preston had more reason than anyone else to want Jerome out of the way. Even if his alibi for the night of the dance was valid, that still didn't mean he was innocent. Jerome might have been killed after he went to Vegas, used the credit cards, and returned to Black Mountain for Heather.

McQuede cut off on a side street and stopped in front of the ruined high school. Because of the darkness and what had taken place here, the scene looked eerie and cruel. Amid still-to-be-removed debris, immobile equipment sat like giant, gloating beasts.

McQuede spotted a black truck parked on the next block, across the street from the fallen building. He wound his way through stacks of rubble toward it.

He stepped to the front, his gaze locking on the dent near the front left headlight. The Ford, old and battered, had been left unlocked. He slipped inside the vehicle, looking around and finding a key in the ashtray. This definitely was the truck that had followed him. But it proved nothing. It would be accessible to practically anyone.

Before he went home, McQuede needed to talk to Fenton and follow up on Heather's complaint. Often he had seen the lights glowing in Fenton's studio, even after midnight, so he'd check there first.

He drove back to Main Street, which looked different now that the businesses had closed for the evening. This time McQuede found the door to Fenton's Studio unlocked.

A bare light bulb overhead cast a gloomy dimness across the room.

"Fenton," he called.

No answer. Fenton had unlocked the shop door and left again, no doubt intending to return soon. McQuede occupied his time by strolling from one framed photo to another. The content of the pictures was somehow unsettling—a ragamuffin kid, hungry and forgotten, standing in a snowdrift; two vicious dogs, fighting to the death, snarling and rolling in a deserted alley. The fact that the photos were in black and white made them even starker. They caused their creator to seem the product of another age, stuck in some ghastly time long past.

Weird, McQuede thought, as he turned to view the pictures hung in disarray on the wall behind him. The one in the center was particularly unnerving: a close-up of a partial face with huge eyes that seemed to be watching him with some deadly intent.

The bell on the door jingled as Fenton, not wearing a jacket and hunched down against the cold, stepped inside. He didn't say anything, just placed the package he was carrying on a desk piled high with boxes.

"I heard about what you found at the old school," Fenton said. He peered at McQuede through his small glasses, his eyes large and frightened. "We're all suspects, aren't we?"

McQuede knew he was going to have to go slowly with Fenton if he were to get any information out of him. He said conversationally, "I'd like to look at some of your pictures from the class of '88."

The bones in his thin shoulders stood out as he bent over a small, three-drawer file box. He began to rummage through it, saying, "I ran across a few a while ago. Yes, here's some."

McQuede shuffled through photographs, finding the one he wanted. Harlan, Fenton, and Ganner were lined up on stage where the Spring Fling Dance had taken place; Jerome, the singer, was holding a guitar and standing slightly out front. Below them Preston and Heather Kenwell stood, side by side and smiling.

"I didn't take that one. Loris did. We were both in photography class. Loris took it at the Homecoming Dance," Fenton said. "Fredrick and Heather were the king and queen."

"If you don't mind, I'll borrow this for a while. You'll get it back." McQuede glanced from the photo to Fenton, and then asked, "When you were taking pictures of the demolition, did you happen to notice an old black truck?"

"Sure. It belongs to Howard Birk."

"Did you ever drive it?"

"No," Fenton replied, and then added, "but he wouldn't care if I did. He lets Harlan use it whenever he has hauling to do."

McQuede placed the photo Fenton had loaned him in his pocket. "I've just been talking to Heather Kenwell," he said.

At the mention of her name, the color drained from

Fenton's face. "She's always complaining about me. I've never done anything to her. I've just tried to help her."

"Help her? Why? She doesn't need your help." McQuede had to come on strong, although he didn't really relish the task. "She doesn't want you taking any more photographs of her."

"The *Black Mountain Herald* buys pictures from me," Fenton said defensively. "She can't say that I can't take them. She's a public figure."

"You were on her property last night. Why were you there?"

"I wasn't. She's always been a liar." He seemed to shrink back as he spoke. He began talking rapidly, in short, choppy sentences. "I know what you're thinking. You're wrong. I'm happily married. I have four children. Heather means nothing to me. She's just a pretty face to photograph. That's all. That's all she's ever been to me."

"You mean you never had a crush on her back in high school?"

"She can have any man she wants. She never looked at me then. She wouldn't now."

"I'm going to warn you, Fenton," McQuede said soothingly. "You'll buy yourself a lot of trouble if you don't stay completely away from her."

As he stood in front of Fenton's Studio, he glanced down the street to The Drifter. It wouldn't hurt, now that he was so close, to question Harlan about the truck and find out the last time Birk had loaned it to him.

Loud music assailed McQuede as he entered the tavern. No one was behind the bar, but the room was crammed, mostly with men from the coal mine. Ruger was dancing with a girl in a very short, black skirt. Aware that all eyes were on her, she tossed back her head and giggled when he spun her around.

When Ruger saw McQuede standing foursquare in the doorway, he stopped with the fancy footwork. "Later, babe," he said to the girl and came forward.

"Where's Harlan?"

"He just left a minute ago. It's me you'll be wanting to address," said Ruger, offering a slight bow. "When he's gone, I'm in charge."

"Have you or Harlan borrowed Birk's truck lately?"

"No, I'm not into heavy labor." Ruger grinned. "Neither is Harlan. He hires out all the hard work."

McQuede had never liked Ruger, the biggest crook in Coal County, and liked him even less with that taunting smile on his face.

"You say he left only a minute ago. Strange I didn't see him leave here."

"He exited by way of the back door," Ruger said.

"Back door, eh? For any particular reason?"

"I suppose he went after a pizza. Cutting through the alley would save him a few steps. What message do you have for him?"

"I'll just talk to him myself." McQuede cut across the small, open space between the bar and the booths.

Ruger's dance partner cooed at McQuede as he walked by her. "You want to dance, handsome? I just love men in uniform."

"I doubt you would like me," he returned. "Ruger doesn't."

He crossed through a back room filled with storage boxes and exited into a very dark alley. He could still hear the blaring music from inside. He stood immobile for a while, and then, thinking he would intercept Harlan as he came back from the pizza parlor, started walking toward the lights.

A *clank* sounded from behind him. Someone must have collided with one of the trash cans that set near the tavern door.

McQuede whirled around. Had Harlan been lying in wait for him out here, or was this Ruger?

A large form emerged from out of the blackness. The figure was clad in a long, dark coat, a ski mask over his face, and like some apparition, it seemed to linger a moment, to float.

Then he charged, so fast that he blurred before McQuede's eyes. He wielded a weapon, an iron pipe or a wrecking bar. Jerome's skull flashed through McQuede's mind.

Before McQuede could make a move, the man reached him. The iron pipe—he could see it clearly now—rose high in the air. At any moment McQuede would feel the impact, the shattering force of iron against his temple.

Chapter Nine

With speed that matched his assailant's, McQuede ducked, blocking the course of the weapon. The pipe smacked against his right arm, striking midway between wrist and elbow. He clamped his lips against the intense pain.

The iron bar, brandished with the fury of a madman, flung upward, ready to strike again. With equal fury, McQuede charged forward, smashing into his attacker full-force. Still clinging to the pipe, the man stumbled backward. McQuede recovered his balance and dived forward, knocking him from his feet. They fell hard, rolling on the hard-packed dirt.

McQuede had the advantage of size, but his opponent possessed a wiry quickness. He broke free and scrambled to his feet. McQuede grabbed his leg and sent him hurling backward. He pinned him to the ground, one hand on his throat, the other ripping away the ski mask.

The man cried out in terror.

"Fenton!" McQuede gasped. "What the hell . . . ?"

McQuede clutched Fenton's arm and dragged him to his feet.

"My glasses. My glasses," he moaned.

McQuede twisted his arms behind his back and snapped on handcuffs. He lifted the ski mask from the ground, shook the glasses free, and stuffed them in Fenton's coat pocket. "I'm booking you for assault," he said breathlessly.

Retrieving the pipe, McQuede pushed Fenton ahead of him toward the squad car. He threw open the door and informed Fenton of his rights as he slid into the backseat.

The pain in McQuede's arm increased his anger. "You rigged that so-called accident at the high school too, didn't you?"

Fenton shrank down in the seat. "No," he whimpered. "I didn't do that. I followed you tonight because it was the only chance I had of getting back what was mine."

"You gave me that photo. Why would you want it back?"

"Not that dance picture," he said with disdain. "The packet you took from my studio. How could you do that? Get into my private file cabinet and steal from me."

"What are you talking about?" McQuede demanded.

"My collection of old photos from my senior year. You took them all, even the negatives." He leaned back against the seat. The shaking that had started in his voice became evident in his thin frame. "You had no right to steal them!" he screeched. "I want them back!"

"Enough to commit another murder?"

"I'm not a killer. I only wanted what was mine to begin with."

McQuede's breath became more even. "I didn't take your packet. All I have is the picture you gave me."

"So you say. But I caught you in my studio. How long had you been in there snooping around before I got back?"

"Those pictures must be very incriminating," McQuede stated. "They link you with Jerome's murder, don't they?"

"I knew you'd think that," Fenton groaned. "Whenever things go wrong, I'm always the one who everyone blames."

"Why would those pictures make me think you had murdered Jerome?"

Fenton remained leaning limply back against the seat. "They didn't concern Jerome. Just Heather."

"Why would that make you look guilty? You're still taking pictures of her."

"My wife . . . my kids . . . Diane would leave me! No one would understand."

"I might."

"Most of the photos were of Heather. No one would grasp my real reason for doing this. They'd think I was . . . crazy about her. But that wasn't the case at all." His voice grew faint, faraway. "Heather's the reason I went into photography. She is and has always been *my* model, the perfect woman for an artist's lens."

"You're not telling me everything. I want a complete description of those photos."

Fenton straightened up in the seat. He stared through the windshield at the deserted street. "Some were . . . not so nice. With Heather . . . not dressed."

"Did Heather consent to your taking those shots of her?"

"No. Heather would sunbathe in that arbor behind her

house. In the nude. I took them . . . without her permission."

"If they are leaked to the press," McQuede noted, "they'll damage Heather's chance of winning the election."

Fenton didn't react to this; it wasn't Heather he was trying to protect. "If people saw them, they'd think I was some sort of pervert. But that's not the case at all. I'm an artist!"

McQuede stared at him. *A sick puppy,* he thought. He'd probably murdered Jerome so Heather would stay here in Black Mountain.

McQuede now faced the impossible task of putting together a twenty-year-old case against Fenton and making it stick. Early the next morning he started toward Las Vegas to trace the route of the credit cards and see where that led him.

Instead of a squad car, McQuede took his Jeep Grand Cherokee. He loved the color, a vermilion red. He loved the way it handled when the roads got rough. But most of all, he loved the fact that it wasn't ten years old, as most of his cars had been.

As McQuede drove, an image of Bruce Fenton remained fastened in his mind. Fenton had probably struck Jerome in a fit of passionate anger, the same way he attacked McQuede last night. After Fenton killed Jerome, he no doubt had panicked. So he took the credit cards, using them to make a trail across country, leading everyone to think Jerome was still alive.

McQuede had made a careful study of the credit card statements. One card was good only at a particular brand of gas station, and the limit had been reached just outside of Vegas. The second one had been used at eating places and motels along the way, ending with a large transaction at Sammy's Place in Las Vegas, where the paper trail ended. The cash transaction at the casino had totally maxed out the second card.

However impossible the task, McQuede would try to find a witness who could remember the person who had used the cards. Once in Vegas, he'd confront Sammy Ratone again, using the picture of the band members to jog his memory.

He drove for hours. Around Rock Springs, the land flattened and became so treeless McQuede could see for miles. He knew this region like the back of his hand, his father and grandfather's country. The much-feared and respected Jeffery McQuede, his distant uncle and namesake, a famous lawman, had in the late 1800s ridden his horse in this area, keeping the peace and tracking down bandits. He too must have known every ridge and hill dotted with sage, the places where the clouds hung over the bluffs and where shadows fell into the depths of the canyon. McQuede himself could pinpoint the very moment the hills would turn from desert tan to a dull rust color.

Oil rigs that hadn't been present in the old sheriff's days dotted the landscape. The one before him, mindlessly pumping, looked like a giant insect, an overgrown praying mantis from some science fiction movie, making the surroundings an alien terrain.

The first place the credit card had been used was a gas station on the edge of Rock Springs. Although Cowboy's

Gas and Go was still operating under the same name, it had probably changed hands several times. McQuede filled his tank and purchased a cup of coffee. The young man at the counter politely studied the picture, even though he had probably been little more than a toddler when someone using Jerome's identity had made the fateful trip.

"I'm sorry I can't help you," he said with a shake of his head. "I've only been here a few months."

McQuede had expected as much. Still, he felt a twinge of disappointment. He pressed on, realizing how futile his efforts probably were, knowing that his questions came twenty years too late.

For some time, McQuede drove the straight ribbon of a road, one he had almost to himself, without stopping. The air grew cooler as he reached a mountainous stretch. The road wound downward into the small town of Lost Pines past the Wyoming border. He checked the statements. Whoever had used the cards had spent some time here, overnight, at a place called Timber Creek, which made Mc-Quede hopeful he could gather some information. Things changed quickly, but in a small community like this, memories were long, especially when it came to strangers. If only the user of the cards had created some kind of stir, maybe ended up in jail, then a mug shot might be kept on file.

McQuede could find no trace of a gas station on the corner of Spruce and Adams called Handy's Full Service. On that spot now stood a slick and modern convenience store.

McQuede filled the tank again, wishing full service wasn't a thing of the past. "This place used to be called

Handy's Full Service a while back," he said as he paid the cashier.

The gray-haired man he addressed was old enough to have been behind the counter twenty years ago. "That's what I've heard. I'm not from around here though. The guy who ran it, Jim Roth, passed away a few years back. The wife and I took it over about then. Moved here from California."

McQuede's discouragement deepened. Even if Jim Roth had still been alive, it had been too long ago to expect him to remember a young man, one of countless people, who had just passed through.

"Ever heard of a restaurant named Frannie's Diner? It's probably gone too."

"Sure, everyone's heard of Frannie's. At least some of the locals still call it that. Only it's changed names. It's the Chef's Delight now."

McQuede checked the local police station and the local bar with no results. As darkness fell, McQuede, getting hungry, stopped in front of the neon sign advertising Chef's Delight.

A young waitress with springy brown hair and a pleasant smile took his order. She wasn't old enough to have been working here when the place had been called Frannie's, but McQuede still asked his questions and received the usual polite shrug and shake of the head.

Resigned, McQuede turned his attention to his food. The coffee, weak and tasting like watered-down mud, made him wish he were back at Mom's Café. He missed his old routine, even more so once he had sampled the tough roast beef and overcooked mashed potatoes. Despite the bad food, he left a generous tip, wondering if Jerome or his impostor had gotten a better meal than he had.

As he paid the check, he paused to ask, "Have you ever heard of the Timber Creek Motel?"

"There used to be a place by that name about five miles west, but it's been boarded up for years."

Maybe it was the forlorn, faded wooden sign still advertising a place that no longer existed that roused McQuede's curiosity, prompting him to take a side trip down the rough, unpaved road that led to Timber Creek. Glad that he had driven his Jeep, McQuede began to climb an unexpectedly steep grade.

The twisting road overlooked a little canyon. Near the top he caught sight of the long-abandoned motel that probably hadn't seen a customer since the days of Jerome Slade. Despite the scenic view, he wondered how, even in its heyday, the motel could have attracted any tourists to this isolated spot.

A blast of cool mountain air billowed his jacket as he got out of the Jeep. Weathered plywood, some with graffiti, had been nailed over the windows. The surrounding darkness, made worse by encroaching pines and firs, added an eerie dimension. He switched on his flashlight and let it slide across the adjoining rooms, settling on the sign above the office, Timber Creek Motel. Nothing could be left of Jerome Slade or his impersonator's visit—just a memory, ghostlike, distant, and reeking with evil.

A door to one of the rooms stood ajar, and he could see where mice and other creatures had done their damage. A once-yellow carpet, faded and water-stained, still clung to the floor. In the corner, scavengers had toppled an old sink and stripped the faucets.

McQuede walked around, kicking at the loose rubble, thinking about how this small room with a once-warm bed and paint the color of sunflowers had been a haven for the weary.

The total desertion reminded him that this whole trip was a waste of time. Abruptly he turned and walked outside. Just as he did, he spotted a vehicle, void of lights, inching along through the trees. The black shadow drew to a momentary stop, then quickly disappeared behind the motel.

McQuede raced to his Jeep. He followed, headlights jogging over the rough ground. By the time he rounded the building, the truck had vanished. He stepped on the brake, trying to detect some movement in the trees, then pulled out onto the road. He looked both ways. To the left a sharp curve blocked his view.

McQuede, guessing the truck hadn't returned to the highway, continued on the winding road, which in less than a mile dropped into a little valley, where an old, two-story house set against the mountain. The yard light illuminated the dark blue paint of a late model truck parked near the entrance. At first McQuede had assumed this had been the dented black Ford following him again, but now he realized it had been a neighbor passing by, one who had stopped out of curiosity to see what he was doing. After McQuede had started his Jeep, they had gone on home.

Relieved, McQuede swung the Jeep around and headed back to the highway. Struck by a basketball scoreboard and chased around by a maniac intent on bludgeoning him—no wonder he was jittery.

Chapter Ten

Anxious to be on his way, McQuede drove another long stretch, stopping only for gas in Cedar City. Growing weary, he pushed on to Vegas.

The road flattened again as he left the mountains, with the grasslands becoming more parched, dry, and treeless as he passed the Nevada border. As he got closer to the big city, cars began to rush past him. Tired, and used to having the road all to himself, McQuede maintained a steady speed as vehicles shot around him.

The lights of Vegas glittered like gemstones in the night sky. McQuede pulled into the nearest hotel, not realizing until he had checked in that it was shabby and run-down, with an air of decadence that could match Sammy's Place. If Loris had been with him, he'd have sprung for one of those fancy hotels along the strip, but tonight he'd settle for this one, conveniently close to Sammy's casino.

McQuede wondered if Loris had been trying to call him, as she had told him she would. He glanced at his watch. It was getting late, but Loris had mentioned that she was a night person. He dialed her number and listened with disappointment to the unanswered rings. She should be home by this time. She was probably out with Ev Ganner.

Sourly, McQuede headed toward the casino. Not finding Sammy, he lingered on the half-balcony in front of his office, which offered an overview of the bottom floor. Below him he watched a gray-haired man putting a hundred dollar bill into a double-diamond machine.

"Strange, isn't it?"

Sammy had come up the stairs and now stood beside him, smiling a little. The continual flashing lights no doubt hurt his eyes, and caused him to don dark-tinted lenses. They seemed to emphasize the puffiness of his face, his large forehead, and heavy jowls.

"Just look at them," he said with satisfaction. "The allure of the machines! What can beat it? No one would come in here and put that much money into my hand."

"If they did," McQuede remarked, "they'd never get it back."

"Ha! You think so little of me," Sammy said. "In truth, I'm much more generous than these machines."

"Ha!" McQuede returned.

Sammy cast him a sideways glance. "A little unpleasant tonight, aren't you?" he asked jovially. "You must have had a hard day. Let's remedy that. Just sit a while in my office, and we'll talk over old times."

McQuede trailed Sammy into the brightly lit room. Sammy eased his short, heavy frame into the plush chair behind his desk and leaned back. He didn't wear a suit jacket tonight, and his shirt gaped open at the throat, revealing matted, black hair.

McQuede regarded him in silence. Sammy had seemed amused by his first visit, but this one appeared to threaten him. Nevertheless, he smiled broadly. "I'm beginning to think you're on my trail for some reason."

Without responding, McQuede seated himself opposite the desk. "Since I talked to you last, a skeleton was uncovered in Black Mountain during the demolition of the old high school."

"And that makes you think of me."

"The victim was identified as Jerome Slade."

Sammy shrugged. "That explains why he didn't show up for that gig I booked for him."

The boy's tragic death meant nothing at all to Sammy. McQuede wondered if Sammy ever saw people as humans or if he just viewed them as scores to settle or money to be made. "Do you make it a habit to employ underage performers?"

"This Jerome Slade you're talking about wasn't going to sing here. I book for places other than gambling joints."

"He, or someone impersonating him, made a trip to Vegas. I've traced the last credit card slips to your casino."

"What can I tell you? The kid never showed up."

"But someone did. And I don't believe in ghosts."

"Do you want a beer?" Sammy asked.

"No, thanks." McQuede shoved the picture of the band in front of Sammy. "I want you to take a look at this. Do any of these faces look familiar?"

Sammy gazed down at Heather, and he smiled again. "Hey, that one's a looker!"

"That's Heather Kenwell. She's running for the senate."

Sammy's pudgy finger came to rest on Bruce Fenton,

then a long-haired boy with thick glasses. "That one. I've seen him a time or two."

McQuede leaned forward. He hadn't really expected Sammy to tell him anything useful. "Are you absolutely sure it was him? A lot of time has passed."

"What do you mean, a lot of time? He was in here just last weekend. He keeps off to himself in some dark corner like he don't want to be seen and plays the slots."

"You're sure this is the same man?"

Sammy chuckled. "This character doesn't have many look-alikes." He glanced at the photo again. "He hasn't changed much, has he? Not the hairstyle, not the glasses. Ha. Talk about being stuck in a time warp. Long-haired then, long-haired now."

Ironic words coming from Sammy Ratone, with his 1930s, small-time gangster appearance.

"Is this the same man who maxed out a credit card at your casino at the time Jerome Slade disappeared?"

"All I know is that I've seen him several times recently. As for who was in here twenty years ago, don't even ask."

McQuede reached for the photo.

"Trouble with you, McQuede," Sammy said, folding his hands across his large stomach, "you're just like this picture. You see things in black and white. You work in a place like Vegas for a while, you begin to see the big picture, the large, gray area."

Sammy had lived his entire life in that gray area, thinking of neither right nor wrong, but of what best served his interests.

McQuede stared at him, wondering where his interests lay now. Ruger and he were mixed up in a lot of rackets, maybe one of them involving Jerome Slade. Sammy always made clear that he didn't deal in drugs, righteous as only the morally bankrupt can be. He seemed, like Ruger, to live by a code that condoned some crimes, while condemning with the fervor of a preacher the sins he wasn't personally guilty of.

Sammy removed his glasses. Without them his eyes lost their protective shield and looked singularly hard.

"You've got it all wrong about me, McQuede," he said affably. "Hey, I'm not really so bad."

"Glad to hear it."

"Old Friend," Sammy called as McQuede started for the door. "I'm going to give you a little advice. Free, of course. Sometimes it don't pay to dig up old bones. If I were you, I'd let the past stay buried in the past."

Out in the hallway, McQuede nearly collided with Sammy's security guard, huge and tough looking, the kind Al Capone might have hired for a hit man. Obviously he had kept post outside Sammy's door, listening. He must be one of the good guys too.

The blue lights of the sign reading MICKEY'S MOTEL, REASONABLE RATES flashed on and off. An extension hanging on a chain beneath announced VACANCY. *Not likely to ever change into NO VACANCY,* McQuede concluded as he pulled into the parking lot.

Once inside, McQuede fell across the bed, fully dressed, boots still on, too exhausted to sleep. The annoying lights through the thin drapes spasmodically intruded into the room.

If only he could find a way to connect Fenton to Jerome's

credit cards, but that wasn't going to happen. Sammy Ratone had been his last hope, and Sammy wasn't talking.

The noisy furnace clicked on. The heat began to make him drowsy, lulling him at last into a half-sleep. The phone jangling beside his bed jolted him fully awake.

Would Loris be returning his call this late? Not likely, but no one knew he was in Vegas except for Sammy, and he sure hadn't told Sammy where he was staying. He lifted the receiver and said, "McQuede."

"I'm warning you, leave the dead undisturbed."

McQuede could barely decipher the strange, distorted voice. The words, muffled and distant, made McQuede think of cold-blooded murder, of a young boy's dashed dreams.

A raspy sound followed, like a sharp intake of breath. Then the caller finished his message with sinister slowness.

"If you don't leave this alone, you will join him."

Chapter Eleven

At the sight of his Jeep, McQuede stopped dead-still. Shards of glass lay shattered on the ground. His gaze moved from the broken headlights to the four slashed tires.

Sammy Ratone had done this! He had threatened him and vandalized his Jeep! Of course, Sammy wouldn't do his own dirty work. McQuede thought of the treacherous-looking gunman who had stood guard in front of Sammy's office, then of Ruger, who could have followed him here.

Sammy's handiwork, no doubt about it! His anger escalated. Then he cautioned himself to go slow. He was condemning him without a shard of proof. He recalled the words of his namesake, the famous Old West lawman who he always tried to emulate, whose bits of advice often sprang from another era to aid him. "When you're convinced you're right, it's time to step back and take another look."

McQuede bent and ruefully inspected the damage to the paint in the area of the broken headlights. He should have invested in the security alarm system the salesman had tried so hard to sell him. Unnecessary in Coal County, where people often left their vehicles unlocked on Main Street, and even though McQuede cautioned them not to, sometimes with the keys hanging in the ignition. The fact that his stereo system remained untouched convinced him this could not be the work of some random vandal, but was related to last night's ominous phone call.

In the motel office he questioned the night clerk, who, like him, had heard and seen nothing. The owner suggested a towing company and a mechanic. While he waited for the repairs to be made, he called the police, and an officer was sent to talk to him. The policeman didn't seem all that interested, just wrote the report and called the office to run a trace on last night's phone call.

The policeman left, and returned some time later. "The call was made from a public phone at Max's Convenience Store. No one there remembered anyone using it."

"Before I got the threatening call, I'd been at Sammy's Place talking to Sammy Ratone. Why don't you check with him and see if he knows anything about this?"

"I'll stop by there."

During the long wait, McQuede paced nervously around the stacks of tires, and then made a call to his deputy, filling him in on what had happened.

"It sounds as if you're getting dangerously close to the truth," said Carlisle. "Better be watching your back."

"I always do," McQuede replied. "Is Bruce Fenton still in custody?"

"You're not going to believe this, but he was out before you even left town. Fredrick Preston showed up right away and put up the bail money. I asked Preston about it, and he said Fenton and he were old chums from high school."

"Check on Fenton now and see if he's in town. By the way, have you talked to Birk about his black pickup?"

"I did. Birk told me it was just an old junker that he lets anyone use. He knew it was gone from the site the day you were being trailed. He said he had loaned it to Loris Conner to haul some items to the museum. I checked fingerprints, but got a jumble of them that won't do us any good."

"I'm more concerned about where it is now."

"Birk tells me he never tries very hard to keep track of it, but I'll talk to him again."

"Ask him specifically if he's ever loaned it to Fredrick Preston." McQuede added, "Did you ask Birk about the gym floor?"

"Yes, he did the work. His records show that the job was done the Wednesday following the dance."

"That would have given Jerome time to go to Vegas and return."

"I also wanted to tell you I checked on Fredrick Preston's alibi as you requested," Sid told him. "He claims his grandson was with him from eleven o'clock until morning. Mr. Preston built up his empire by having a solid reputation. I think he's telling the truth."

"Fredrick Preston might well have an alibi for the night of the dance," McQuede said, "but Jerome may have been murdered a few days later."

"How long will you be in Vegas?"

"I'll be back this evening," McQuede said.

"Be careful."

After an aggravating wait at the repair shop and dissatisfaction with the job done, McQuede got back on the road by late afternoon. He would be driving far into the night.

He arrived at Lost Pines about suppertime. *Better the devil you know than the one you don't,* he thought, as he pulled the Jeep into a parking space in front of Chef's Delight. A waitress about his own age with the same light brown hair and pleasant smile as the young girl who had served him earlier took his order. He wondered if the younger waitress he had spoken to on his way to Vegas might be her daughter.

"I'd recommend the fried chicken," she suggested. "The beef's tough as shoe leather."

"How long have you worked here?" McQuede asked.

She looked at him curiously, as if she had mistaken his question for interest in her.

"Forever," she replied and giggled like a schoolgirl. "My husband passed away in a trucking accident when our daughter was just a baby. When I started working here the place was still called Frannie's."

McQuede leaned closer. Once again she seemed to misread his interest. "Do you have time to talk to me?"

With another giggle and a glance back over her shoulder to the counter, she said, "It's about time for my break." She seated herself opposite him, beaming as if he were a movie star.

Her admiring attention made him uncomfortable. He took the black-and-white photograph from his pocket. "Do any of these faces look familiar?"

"Is this your band?"

"No, I'm a law officer. One of these people came through here in the spring of 1988."

"I must be looking my age," she said and laughed. "Do you have any idea how many people stop here, especially in the summer?"

"I realize I'm grasping at straws."

"You can grasp at me anytime."

He overlooked the offer. "Do you recall a motel named the Timber Creek?"

"Yes, Al Kurtz ran it for years, but it's been closed a long time. Al and his daughter, Sandy, still live on that old road, just about a mile past the abandoned building."

"Thanks. It's a long shot, but I'll check with them."

"I'll call and let them know you're on the way."

She returned to his booth and stayed with him until he had finished his last cup of coffee. He left a big tip and told her the next time he was in Lost Pines he'd stop again.

McQuede's headlights cut through misty darkness as once more he turned down the road toward the old motel. As he passed it, he thought once again of the pickup truck and weighed the possibility that he had been followed from Black Mountain.

The old house, despite the new truck out front, looked like a relic from the past. He waited impatiently after ringing the bell.

A stooped, white-haired man opened the door. "Mr. Kurtz?" McQuede said. "Sorry to disturb you this time of evening."

"Quite all right. We don't get many visitors anymore," Kurtz said, as if the unexpected call were a diversion from long, quiet evenings. With slow and careful steps, he made his way back to an easy chair and gestured for McQuede to sit on the sofa. He put up a brave front, but the paleness of his skin and the deep furrows around his eyes and mouth told McQuede that he was ill and in pain.

"My daughter, Sandy, is brewing some coffee. She's been staying with me since she and her husband split up. I've been stowed up here since my hip surgery. Don't know what I'd do without her help."

An attractive, middle-aged woman with bleached blond hair poked her head around the corner, called a cheery hello, and disappeared back into the kitchen. The way her father's eyes lit up at the sight of her told McQuede that she was the apple of his eye.

McQuede explained about the photograph and showed it to the elderly man. He waited hopefully as Mr. Kurtz put on his glasses and thoughtfully studied the picture. He returned it with a shake of his head.

"My daughter might have been minding the desk that night though," he said. "When was it? '88? She was just out of high school then."

At that moment, Sandy came in with the coffee, a big smile on her face. "Honey, you recognize any of the fellows in this picture?"

Sandy set down the tray and regarded the photo.

McQuede leaned forward, anxiously awaiting her answer. She certainly wasn't going to point out Bruce Fenton, for there wouldn't be any chance that he'd be able to impersonate a rock star. On the other hand, Fredrick Preston could. He might have used Jerome's credit card to cover up his crime.

Sandy's smile suddenly faded. "Oh, I remember Jerome Slade, all right. The louse!"

A young man passing through town would be, and had

been, virtually ignored or forgotten, except in the memory of a once-young girl looking for romance. "So you remember Jerome Slade," McQuede repeated.

"As if I'd ever forget him!" Her bowlike lips, heavy with makeup, tightened. "Fed me some line about being a big rock star with this band called Orion. Just swept me off my feet." Her voice broke. "He asked me out that night, wanted me to show him the town. Only my idea of a good time and his weren't the same, if you get my drift."

"Sandy's a nice girl," her father chimed in proudly, talking about her as if she were still some naive teenager, not a middle-aged woman.

"Mind telling me what happened?"

"We got into a tussle. He acted like some kind of fiend. I fought him hard. I managed to get out of his car and began running. I ran for miles and miles, all the way back here, in the dark and rain. End of story!"

But the look in her eyes told McQuede it wasn't the end of the story, or at least it wasn't the entire story.

Tears formed in her eyes. She wiped them away angrily. "Seeing that awful face brings it all back. Just like it was yesterday." Her voice had changed now and sounded like that of a frightened little girl. "The way he grabbed at me, hands all over, tearing at my clothes. I was scared to death! He was so strong. I had bruises all over my arms and neck from fighting him off."

Blue veins stood out on Al Kurtz's temple, and his face turned as white as his hair. "Why didn't you tell me?" he asked angrily. "I'd have taken care of that scoundrel then and there!"

McQuede felt pity for the young girl who must have had illusions that this would-be rock star was her knight on a white horse, the answer to her dreams.

"I was too ashamed, Daddy." She looked away, and her voice trembled as she continued. "I was afraid you'd be upset with me for sneaking out after my curfew. So I just crept back into my room and cried myself to sleep."

Mr. Kurtz reached over and patted her arm. "Poor little darling."

"That was a long time ago, Daddy. Nothing for you to worry about now."

Sandy's eyes met McQuede's over her father's frail form, and suddenly McQuede read between the lines. What had actually taken place that night was far worse than she had told.

Bitter resentment shone in her eyes. "What happened to him? I hope something bad! That creep, with his big ego and those stupid tattoos."

"Tattoos?" McQuede echoed, puzzled. He handed her the photograph again. "Which one of these is Jerome Slade?"

"Oh, I'll never forget that face." Decisively she pointed, not at Jerome Slade, but at Harlan Daniels.

"Are you certain?"

"That's him, all right! And I'd do anything to bring him down."

McQuede felt a jolt as reality sank home. Jerome Slade had been killed the night of the dance as he had first believed. And Harlan Daniels, not Bruce Fenton, had taken Jerome's credit cards and made this trip impersonating him. And that meant McQuede had found the killer.

He had not actually expected anyone to recall a young man briefly passing through so long ago, but he had underestimated the memory of a woman so cruelly mistreated. Sandy Kurtz could not only identify Harlan and tie him directly to a credit card transaction at the Timber Creek, she would be willing to testify.

Harlan must have followed him Tuesday from Black Mountain. He'd been waiting at the Timber Creek in the black truck because he'd known where McQuede would be heading. Harlan had made the threatening call to his room last night. He'd killed Jerome on some shady deal gone wrong.

McQuede left the Kurtz home quickly and swung his Jeep onto the main road, anxious to get back to Black Mountain. He must arrest Harlan before he realized McQuede was after him. Anticipation caused McQuede's foot to hold hard to the gas pedal. He was only miles away from apprehending Jerome's killer.

Even The Drifter was closed by the time McQuede arrived back at Black Mountain Pass, but a faint light glowing behind the shaded window told him that someone was still inside. McQuede, finding the door unlocked, burst into the tavern, startled to find, not Harlan Daniels, but Ruger behind the counter, getting ready to close for the night.

"Where's Harlan?" he demanded.

"Your guess is as good as mine." Ruger leaned one elbow on the bar, looking as satisfied as a beggar who had just been given a new kingdom. "He called me early Tuesday and asked if I could run things a while."

Tuesday, the day McQuede had left for Vegas.

Ruger's gray eyes, the color of a smoke-filled room, studied McQuede with mild curiosity. "Are you going to arrest him?"

"I just want to talk to him."

McQuede's answer sparked an amused light in Ruger's eyes. "Like you're always wanting to talk to me."

McQuede drew forward and sank down on one of the stools. Ruger, turning his back to him, went on with his cleaning. "Where do you think he is?"

"He might have gone into hiding. Harlan does that once in a while." The usual hint of derision faded from Ruger's voice as he turned back to McQuede. "Harlan often gets threats."

"So do I."

"So I hear."

Ruger must have talked to Sammy and heard about the call made to his motel room.

Ruger's gaze held McQuede's for a long time before he added in an ominous way, "The difference between you and Harlan is he's smart enough to take them seriously."

"Why would anyone threaten him?"

"Some people resent being on the downside of one of his underhanded deals."

"Like you, for instance?"

"We don't have any deals."

"I'd like to know the names of some of these threat-givers. Maybe you could help me out?"

Ruger, who had been rubbing a cloth against the marble counter, stopped all motion. "Prying isn't my style."

"It is mine," McQuede said. "I want to know exactly what Harlan said to you before he left."

"He didn't say much, but he's been acting very strange as of late. He must have liked Jerome a lot. Ever since you found that body, he's been down in the dumps. Keeps reminiscing about that old band of his. Orion."

"The one you were supposed to manage. What can you tell me about that?"

Ruger smiled, catlike. "Oh, it was a band, all right. A band of thieves. They were involved in all sorts of illegal activities."

"Which you and Sammy had nothing to do with."

"You've got that right."

McQuede slid from the bar stool. Harlan had returned to Black Mountain Pass; in fact, McQuede had a strong feeling Ruger had just talked to him.

"Talk has it, he's been wanting to leave Black Mountain." Ruger languidly began to polish the bar again. "You know, I rather like running this place. Maybe I'll see if it's up for sale."

McQuede lingered in front of The Drifter until Ruger switched off the lights. He watched as Ruger checked the door to make sure it was locked, then got into a fancy sports car and drove away. Once Ruger was out of sight, McQuede drove up and down the deserted streets of Black Mountain, determined to find Harlan if it took all night.

He checked the small house where Harlan lived. The door was locked and no vehicle was parked in the drive. He must have slipped in and out of town like a ghost.

Once again McQuede slowed as he drove past The Drifter. He'd been sure the building had been dark when

Ruger left, but now he could detect a light from inside. He pulled to a stop and jumped out.

The front door was locked. He pounded on it, then went around to the back alley where Fenton had attacked him. The back door stood ajar. If Harlan had been here, he'd spotted McQuede and slipped out the back entrance.

Or maybe he was still inside. This could be a trap, with Ruger or Harlan lying in wait, knowing McQuede would return here. McQuede halted, scanning the dark shadows of the alley. He stepped cautiously forward, half-expecting some form to emerge from the blackness, wearing a ski mask and lifting a pipe.

McQuede pushed the door wide open. Not hearing or seeing anyone inside, he moved furtively toward the bar. His gaze fell on the counter, then dropped to the wooden floorboards beneath it. The sight of a big, heavy boot made him stop in his tracks. Recovering, McQuede stepped closer until he could see the other boot, then the crimson pool of blood and shards of shattered glass. The body lay prone upon the floor, tattooed arms sprawled to the side. He had found Harlan Daniels, but he wouldn't be talking. Blood streamed from a shard of glass that stuck out of the jugular vein of his throat, leaving a jagged gash as if he had been attacked by some savage animal.

Chapter Twelve

Early the next morning, McQuede still remained at The Drifter. Ruger arrived early. McQuede could hear his protests, but the deputy who guarded the entrance wouldn't allow him to enter. McQuede stepped outside and faced him across the line of yellow tape.

Ruger looked at him silently, gray eyes unreadable. No regretful laments, no questions about Harlan's murder, just, "How long will the place have to stay closed?"

McQuede ignored the question. "After you left here last night, did you return for any reason?"

"No, I went right home. A full day's work makes a man tired."

"What did you do with the money you took in?"

Ruger patted the thick pocket of his jacket. "I sure didn't leave it here for the lowlifes to steal."

Just like Sammy, Ruger never considered himself one of them. "Did anyone who came in here yesterday act suspicious?"

"Did anyone come in that didn't? Misfits, hoodlums,

that's who hangs out here. If you want my opinion, one of them saw the lights on late at night and thought Harlan was tallying up the day's take."

"That's not what happened," McQuede said sharply.

"Then I'll give you another suggestion. I'll tell you what my ma used to tell me—'those who live by the sword, die by the sword,' or something to that effect. Harlan spent his whole life with his hand on a sword. What more can I tell you?"

If Ruger had stabbed Harlan himself, or even if he could name the killer, McQuede knew he would never get that information out of him. He turned back to the bar.

"If I remember anything that might be of help," Ruger's voice drifted after him, "I'll let you know."

"I'm sure you will." McQuede closed the door between them and remained, assessing once again the scene before him.

Even if McQuede hadn't known this crime was linked in some way Jerome's death, he still wouldn't have thought this the work of a robber. Clearly the killer was someone Harlan knew. He, or rather both of them, had been having a drink at the table near the bar. Two glasses remained there, one of them tipped on its side. McQuede drew forward, smelling the whiskey from the overturned glass, noting how one of the chairs lay on its back on the floor.

Harlan had left his companion, for his body had been found at the end of the bar. McQuede traced his steps. Blood everywhere, on the floor, the counter, the wall—the scene of a terrible fight.

The bottle, used as a murder weapon, had been slammed against the edge of the counter and broken. Fragments still remained. McQuede knelt beside the base, half-filled with dark liquid, and was again assailed by the strong smell of whiskey.

He rose slowly. Years ago, and maybe even recently, former members of Orion had been involved in local robberies. This could be the end result, but that wasn't the only possibility. To convince the townspeople that Jerome was still alive, Harlan could have been hired by the real killer to leave a trail of Jerome's credit cards. If so, when McQuede began to close in on him, Harlan had decided not to take the blame and had made the mistake of saying as much to the person who had hired him.

But what about the photographs stolen from Fenton's studio? Had they all been of Heather, or had one of them been of Jerome's killer? If so, Harlan might have stolen Fenton's pictures for his own profit, to use for blackmail.

"I can't believe it."

McQuede swung around.

Ev Ganner, looking exceptionally pale, light hair ruffled, stood rigidly in front of the cash register. He started toward McQuede, but as if struck by a sudden illness, slowed his step, groping the top of the bar for support.

"Don't touch anything," McQuede ordered, then tried to soften his words by explaining, "No one's supposed to be in here. This place hasn't been dusted for prints yet."

Ganner, seeming even more ill, dropped large hands to his sides as if he no longer knew what to do with them. "I'm sorry. I asked your deputy if I could talk to you, and he told me to go on in." He glanced around at the blood, his gaze falling to the chalk marks on the floor. "I rushed right over the minute I heard. I thought I could be of some help to you."

McQuede studied him.

"Even though life took us in different directions," Ganner said, "Harlan always remained my friend. This is quite a blow to me. You never expect your old high school chums to die like this."

"There's bound to be a link between his death and that band, Orion."

"I knew even back then, as a kid, that I had gotten in with the wrong crowd," Ganner replied. "I did have the good sense to be the first to leave."

"What caused you to make that decision?"

"Harlan and Jerome were coming up with crazy schemes to make fast money. I didn't want any part of it. I warned Bruce to get out too, but he stayed on for several months after I quit the band."

"Were they fencing goods to Sammy Ratone and Ruger?"

"I can't tell you that."

"Did Harlan attend that spring dance?"

"I'm not sure. I left early."

"What time?" McQuede asked. "Do you remember?"

"By eleven I was in bed sound asleep. I headed home because I wasn't having any fun. No one was getting along. Everyone was talking about Jerome and Heather and whether or not they would carry out their plans to elope, and, frankly, I didn't care."

"Everyone? Do you think Senator Kenwell knew they were going to leave Black Mountain that night?"

"Sure, and Fredrick too."

"Would either of them have tried to stop them from going off together?"

Whether he knew the answer to that or not, Ganner did not comment.

"How did Preston deal with her ditching him for Jerome?"

"No one ever knows how Fredrick is going to react, or how anyone is, for that matter. I couldn't believe it when I heard Bruce had attacked you. I was even more surprised when Fredrick jumped in and bailed him out of jail."

"They were classmates, same as you," McQuede reminded him.

"But not friends. In fact, Fredrick tormented Bruce all through school. He's the one who tagged that label on him, Freaky Fenton. Heather encouraged him, of course, and together they made Bruce's life completely miserable."

"Did Preston poke fun at Jerome too?"

"No one trifled with Jerome because Heather was crazy about him. I was never sure, though, whether Jerome felt the same way about her."

"So you think Jerome might have changed his mind about leaving with her that night?"

"That's a possibility. Jerome did have his choice of girls, and those kinds are always finding someone they like better. He probably didn't, though. The Kenwell name reeks of money, and that's what he wanted."

"From what I hear, Heather's father doted on her. He could have tried to interfere with their leaving Black Mountain together."

"Senator Kenwell seemed a decent man," Ganner replied, "but no one really knows what a father will do when it comes to protecting his daughter."

That could work both ways, McQuede thought. He was convinced Heather would do anything in her power to avoid a public scandal. It could be her turn, now, to protect her father's name.

Ganner then added, as if he'd just been hit by a startling revelation, "This crime didn't have to be committed by a man. The killer could be a woman."

Harlan had been killed between midnight and 1:00 A.M. so, without any delay on his part, McQuede began checking on the whereabouts of his suspects. The first one that sprang to mind was Heather Kenwell.

When McQuede left The Drifter, he spotted Ruger leaning against his car talking on a cell phone. As he started by him, Ruger gestured for him to stop.

"Got an old friend of yours on the line. He wants to talk to you."

"Who?"

In answer Ruger passed the phone to him.

Sammy Ratone's affable voice rang loud and clear. "You're going to be real pleased when I tell you the news. I'm on the road right now, headed for Black Mountain."

"Somehow that doesn't thrill me. What's going on?"

"I'm closing a deal on The Drifter. I'll be the new owner, and Ruger will be my manager."

"How does that happen? Harlan Daniels has only been dead for a matter of hours."

"Ruger will fill you in on the details. Ha! All I wanted was your blessing."

"Blessing denied."

"Ha!"

McQuede handed the phone back to Ruger.

"I'll call you back." Ruger, smiling, slipped his phone into his jacket pocket. "You look puzzled, McQuede, so I'll fill you in. About three weeks ago, the bank foreclosed on Harlan and now has full ownership. Harlan's just been using his allotted time to close out."

"That's the first I heard of this."

"With Harlan dead, I thought I'd just take a stroll down to the bank and talk to Fredrick Preston. He's more than happy to close a deal with Sammy . . . at our convenience."

"You don't waste much time grieving, do you?"

Ruger's smile appeared again. "You always twist the facts so I sound like a rogue, which I'm not. Harlan simply threw his torch to me."

"We'll see how long you keep it burning."

The two men had probably always been playing out their crooked schemes here, but McQuede found this news unsettling. The invasion of Sammy Ratone into Coal County, having a small-time crime syndicate right under his nose—that spelled big-time trouble.

Chapter Thirteen

McQuede drove slowly out of town. The stately walls of the Kenwell home rose like a barrier in the distance.

A very formal, gray-haired housekeeper answered the door.

"Is Heather Kenwell home?"

"No, but Mrs. Greg Kenwell is in the study. I can find out from her when Ms. Kenwell will return."

"Maybe I can talk to her instead."

"Just a moment." The woman left and soon returned. "Mrs. Kenwell will see you. This way, please."

McQuede was admitted into a magnificent study where a regal-looking lady, one he had seen only in newspapers, sat at a huge desk. Behind her, huge marble sculpted heads of Washington and Lincoln were set on either side of a giant bookcase.

Heather's mother extended a thin hand. McQuede had expected her grip to be languid, but found it surprisingly firm. "I've heard so much about you. I'm glad to be meeting you."

111

McQuede liked her smile, which held no hint of duplicity or snobbishness. Though she resembled her daughter physically, she seemed far more gracious and elegant.

"Please make yourself comfortable."

McQuede eased himself down into a chair, sinking into soft cushions.

Her kindly manner put him at ease. She had a way of appraising him as if she could see through all facades to the truth.

"I always wanted Greg to support your campaigns," she said pleasantly, "but he referred to you as too much of a 'cowboy,' whatever that means."

McQuede chuckled. "That's a backdoor compliment."

"I thought so. That's why I've always voted for you." She leaned back in the chair, her smile fading slowly. "I'm sorry you can't talk to Heather. She works on her campaign day and night. She's so exhausted when she comes in. Last night she went to her room before the ten o'clock news."

McQuede wondered if she had stated this purposefully, so he wouldn't have to ask where Heather had been at the time Harlan was killed.

"Your case, is it going well?"

"Harlan Daniels was stabbed last night at The Drifter. I'm afraid what happened to him is linked to Jerome Slade's death. That's why I'm here. I need to find out a little more about Heather's relationship with Jerome."

"The boy found no favor with my husband, but I always thought Jerome had . . . potential."

"I take it your husband opposed Heather's seeing him?"

"I'll be truthful with you," Mrs. Kenwell said. "Jerome asked for Greg's permission to marry Heather, and Greg told him to stay away from her. Heather tried in every way to persuade him otherwise. I still shudder at those terrible fights." She faltered and looked away from him. "Greg was so headstrong, and so is Heather."

"Did Jerome bring Heather home from the spring dance that night?"

"No. Greg had gotten wind of their plans to elope. He insisted that she leave the dance with us, around eleven or eleven-thirty. Heather ran up to her room and slammed the door. We didn't hear her leave, but sometime before midnight, she packed some of her belongings and set off to meet him."

"I suppose Heather took it hard when Jerome didn't show up."

"She never once condemned Jerome—it was her father she blamed. For a long time she refused to even talk to him. I didn't know what to do. Heather was so devastated. The poor child could hardly be persuaded to leave her room."

"Sounds like my first experience with love," McQuede said, trying to lighten the mood.

"If it hadn't been for that dear boy, Fredrick, I don't know what would have become of her. He stood by her in true Preston style."

"It's sad that their marriage didn't last," McQuede replied.

"Heather left him twice before they finalized their divorce."

"I've talked to Preston about Heather. He complained about the way she ran through his money."

Mrs. Kenwell smiled. "She ran through our money, not his. After they were married, her daddy kept paying her bills. Greg didn't think supporting her was his duty any longer, not with all the Preston money she had married into, but, regardless, he continued to give her all she wanted. He wouldn't have minded at any other time, but during those years Greg was having big financial reverses."

"That surprises me."

"The higher the climb, the harder the fall," she replied. "Do you remember Billy Osterman? I know you've seen that vacant packing plant between here and Durmont— my reminder not to buy into anyone's wild schemes."

"Osterman took advantage of a lot of people," Mc-Quede said. "Then he declared bankruptcy and left the country."

"Greg usually made such solid investments, but every once in a while he was prone to back what he called 'a plunger.' Billy Osterman fit that bill. He convinced Greg this was a perfect place for his operation, and it would have been had Billy Osterman possessed any degree of business sense. He put up the most expensive buildings, bought the finest equipment. Then one day our lawyer called and said, 'I hope you didn't invest too much with Billy Osterman. He's declaring bankruptcy and letting his investors eat the losses.'"

"What year did this take place? Do you recall?"

Mrs. Kenwell rose. Quick, lithe hands ruffled through a filing cabinet where she extracted a file and handed it to him. "He left here November 1987."

Nineteen eighty-seven, McQuede thought with surprise. Fredrick Preston had told him he had lost his graduation gift of sixty thousand dollars by investing with Osterman. Very strange, indeed, when the plant closed its doors in

November, six months before Preston had received that graduation gift from his grandfather.

"I'd like to have a copy of this transaction, if it's not too much trouble."

McQuede had to wait in the bank lobby until Fredrick Preston was free to talk to him. Once he was summoned, he hurried up the steps to his office and tossed the file Mrs. Kenwell had copied for him on Preston's desk.

"What is this?"

"You lied to me," McQuede said. "You never lost any money in dealings with Billy Osterman."

Preston pushed the papers aside and rose angrily. "I've had enough of your prying into my affairs. There's absolutely no call for it! My standing in this community—"

"—doesn't make a bit of difference to me," McQuede finished Preston's sentence. "What did you do with the sixty thousand your grandfather gave you?"

"I don't have to account to you for what I do with my money." Preston got to his feet challengingly. "Now, will you please leave my office?"

"If I can't get that information from you," McQuede said quickly, "I'll use other sources to find out. The first thing I'm going to do is talk to your grandfather."

Preston looked trapped, like a robber caught with his hand in the till. As usual, he must have confided in his grandfather, and he realized now that his grandfather, if asked, would tell the truth.

Preston sank back down, running a hand through his thick, black hair. He didn't look up at McQuede. "It's like I said before, Heather ran though it."

"Mrs. Kenwell just told me otherwise. And so did Heather."

Preston stared at the file for a while, then said solemnly, almost contritely, "When I told you that, I just wanted to steer you away from what I'd done. I never once thought you'd question my answer."

"You should have invented a better story then, one that wouldn't be proven wrong so easily."

"I answered you on impulse. I remembered how Mr. Kenwell had lost a huge amount of money on that plant, so I thought it would work for my excuse too. I guess I miscalculated—both the year Osterman left town, and you."

"Why don't you tell me what you really did with your money?"

Preston, still not looking up from the desk, replied, "Whenever he looked at Heather, Jerome Slade saw dollars. Heather was willing to leave her Daddy's backing and run off with him, but that wasn't enough for him. It would have been enough for me, even if I hadn't had a nickel to my name."

"So you turned the money over to Jerome and made a deal with him to get out of Black Mountain and to leave Heather behind."

"All Jerome really wanted was Vegas and a music career, and I knew it." Preston looked up at McQuede then, his dark eyes filled with misery. "What I really wanted was Heather."

McQuede gazed at him skeptically. "So Heather was going to leave you, and you couldn't allow that to happen. The only problem is, I have no way of knowing that

Jerome took your offer. It's just as likely that you two fought and that you buried him at that construction site."

"I've never resorted to violence to achieve any goal," Preston said soberly. "Money has always bought me every-thing I want."

McQuede felt a moment's prompting to believe him.

"I gave Grandfather's gift to Jerome Slade, all right," Preston stated bitterly. "The worst deal I ever made. I spent all that money to get Heather. I should have bought that sports car instead."

Chapter Fourteen

McQuede picked up the telephone receiver, his spirits immediately lifting at the sound of Loris' voice. She had called at last! He felt a little disappointed when she said, "Jeff, don't forget the benefit at the museum tonight. You're going to be there, aren't you?"

McQuede had been so busy he had forgotten that the event was scheduled for this evening. "Wouldn't miss it," he said.

This probably didn't count as a real date. Or did it? Did Loris really want him to attend, or had she only invited him out of politeness? In any event, he wasn't going to ignore a chance to spend the evening in Loris' company, even if he had to share her with a crowd of historians and museum enthusiasts.

McQuede shaved the two-day growth of stubble from his chin, tamed his dark hair, and finished with just a spritz, not too much, of aftershave. Then he put on his best jacket, the one he always imagined made him seem an inch taller, his shoulders a bit broader. It promised to be a good evening, and he could use one, a diversion from all the turmoil that had gone on this week.

The benefit was being held in the small auditorium that adjoined the main museum area. People clustered in groups or sat at tables decorated with fancy lace cloths. McQuede looked around for Loris, but didn't see her. He paused to help himself to the coffee, then made an attempt to mingle. Tonight he was out of uniform, but a sheriff was never really off duty, never just one of the crowd. Conversations often stopped when he approached, people checked their words, even their grammar, as if McQuede might have the power to arrest them for saying *ain't.*

Feeling a little like an outsider, McQuede wandered over to where Bernie Slade was standing, near the raffle box. The old man squinted at the poster of *Stampede* that portrayed the painting Loris wanted to purchase for the museum.

"Can't say as I think much of that picture," Bernie said.

McQuede stopped beside him, looking askance at the brilliant, whirling lines and the disembodied buffalo eyes and hooves.

"But I'm sure enough going to take my chances on that prize." Bernie dug out a creased five-dollar bill and handed it to the volunteer who was manning the booth.

Probably his last five dollars, McQuede thought.

"Remember, you have to be here at nine o'clock to win," the attendant said jovially. "Otherwise they'll draw another ticket, and you'll forfeit the prize money."

Bernie peered closely at the paper stub. The hopeful look on his face made McQuede smile. Bernie had put on a clean, though rumpled, shirt, and to McQuede's surprise, he appeared sober. He wasn't a bad sort when he wasn't drunk. Although he had pretended not to care, McQuede knew that the news of his estranged son's death had hit him hard. Perhaps it was the knowledge that he had nobody now that made him seem older, frailer.

Bernie said wistfully, "Hope I got the lucky number. Five hundred dollars sure would come in handy about now."

"Extra cash always does," McQuede agreed. His raffle ticket, which he had purchased from Loris earlier, was still tucked into his wallet.

Bernie stuffed his ticket into a pocket, suddenly dejected. "Probably just wasted my fiver. I've been a loser all my life. Why would I think I'd have a chance at this stupid raffle?"

"Luck's a funny thing though, isn't it?" McQuede responded. "Like gold, the strike comes when it's least expected."

"You're right there," Bernie said, cheering up a little. From the assortment of desserts on the buffet table, he selected a paper plate overflowing with chocolate cake. Crumbs sprinkled across his faded shirt as he pinched off a bite with his fingers. "I'm not willing to lay down and die yet, not when there's still good food to eat and prizes to be won."

McQuede had to admire his spunk. He always liked a survivor.

Through the wide-open double doors, McQuede spotted Loris talking to Preston and Ganner in the center of the museum. It seemed the three of them were always in a huddle, but since they had gone to school together, their memories and friendship went back a long way.

Loris turned and smiled at him. She looked stunning this evening in a turquoise-colored blouse and multicolored, flowing skirt. Dangling gold earrings set off the glow in her honey-colored hair. As McQuede wound through the crowd toward her, Preston's dark eyes darted to him, unwelcomingly.

"Everyone's getting tickets for the raffle," Loris said excitedly. "And a couple of our regular supporters have pledged big donations. We should have enough money to purchase *Stampede*."

"Good idea to buy one of his paintings while they're affordable," Preston said. "Carlo Owatah's work is climbing in value every year."

"I knew he was slated for fame," Loris responded. "That's why I purchased my painting, *Night Spirit*, when he was still unknown."

McQuede remembered the disturbing painting of the warrior—the fierce image of a face suspended against a red and black sky—when it had hung in the Spence Gallery. Like the buffalo stampede, it wasn't anything he fancied.

"I can't tell you how many people have offered to buy it," Loris went on. "Of course, I'd never sell my precious Carlo."

McQuede thought about Sammy Ratone and how he always tried to buy the works of this painter, not because Sammy loved art, but for the profit he made by turning them over to wealthy collectors.

Preston broke in, anxious to return to previous business. "How are things coming along with the plans for the reunion?"

Ganner explained to McQuede, "Loris was talking to

us earlier. She wants Fredrick and me to help her plan a big blowout for the Class of '88."

"Some won't want to hold it this year after all that's happened," Loris said, "but Jerome wouldn't have been one of them."

"He'd have loved the fancy stage in our new school," Ganner remarked.

"We can make this reunion a kind of tribute, a memorial to Jerome," Loris went on brightly. Her joy was forced, only on the surface. She reminded McQuede of someone trying not to cry at a funeral.

"We have to locate some pictures of him," she said. "Do you have any?"

Both classmates shook their heads.

McQuede had found out photos of Jerome Slade were rare, mostly restricted to the class yearbooks. Mementos generally came from family—he doubted Bernie had ever owned a camera, and Jerome had no doting mother to record the milestones of his young life—his first step, his first day of school, the first date.

"I thought we could also have another table spread with snapshots of our senior year. Bruce should be able to supply us with some. He's such a good photographer. He's always clicking that camera, so he's probably got plenty of them." Loris glanced around the room, then asked, "Does anyone know if Bruce is here tonight?"

Fenton had probably stayed away, McQuede thought, to avoid seeing him.

"I heard there was a break-in at his studio. Some of his pictures turned up missing," Preston told her. He fixed McQuede with an icy stare. "You know how much Bruce loves his photos. He's probably sunk into a deep depression, so we won't be seeing him for a while."

"They couldn't be of value to anyone but him." Loris glanced questioningly at McQuede. He realized Fenton's savage attack on him had not gotten back to Loris, at least not yet.

"We're still looking into it," McQuede replied.

"I still have some copies that Bruce gave me," Loris said. "They were mostly of basketball events and dances. I think I stored the box in the basement, at least I tucked them away somewhere." She glanced at Ganner and Preston. "What kind of photos would you like to see displayed?"

"Shots of our old cars," Preston said, lightening up a bit. "I'll never forget that big, white rust-bucket Chevy of Bruce's." He smiled. "You could hear the muffler rattling clear down the street." He turned to Ganner. "And what about that old, yellow VW bug you used to drive? Did you keep any pictures of that contraption?"

"No," Ganner said, a sudden coolness in his voice.

Preston seemed not to notice. "That's a shame. A poor-man's limousine, a real relic."

"We didn't all have rich daddies like you did," Ganner said curtly.

Preston's words sparked tension between the two. McQuede sensed a hint of petty resentment and jealousy that probably had its roots in high school when, no doubt, they sat at different tables, separated by money and popularity.

In the small sphere of high school, things take on a certain order, McQuede thought, that often lasts a lifetime. Some, like Fenton, still lived in the past; others, like Preston and Heather, forever strived to maintain their class presidencies and homecoming king and queen status.

"By the way, what happened to that cherry red Datsun you were so dead set on buying?" Ganner asked suddenly.

The question seemed to momentarily catch Preston off guard. Quickly recovering, he said, "*She* happened." Preston glared at his well-dressed ex-wife, who stood amid a cluster of fans a short distance away.

The embroidered designer jacket, threaded with gold, that embellished the chic black dress Heather wore would probably have cost a month of McQuede's pay.

As if his pride were injured, Preston boasted, "But I'm doing quite well now that she's no longer such a drain on my income. I may not have gotten the car I wanted then, but I can't complain about my brand-new silver Cadillac."

As if aware she were being discussed, Heather started toward them. "May I join the party?" she asked sweetly.

"We're just going over plans for the reunion," Preston said.

"Do we have to have it at the school?" she asked. "It's too bad we have to include *everyone* in this reunion. Otherwise, we could throw a big bash at the Country Club." She cast a smug glance at Preston as if the two of them, despite their differences, were still allies. "Can you imagine Freaky Fenton in *black tie*?" She laughed. "Some people just never did fit in with our crowd." As she spoke, Heather's gaze lighted on Loris, sending the subtle message that if she had her way, Loris too would be excluded.

Loris ignored her.

McQuede silently observed the key members of the class of '88, which had shown up in full force. He was aware of the complicated relationships, the friendships and animosities between them. Now, all grown up, had they kept the same loyalties? Were they still capable of uniting in a common interest? Or had only one of them planned and carried out the murder of Jerome Slade?

"We're looking for photos of Jerome," Loris said, her gaze leveled on Heather. "Maybe you could help us out."

"I tore all mine up a long time ago," Heather returned. "And you should have too." She spun and stalked off, expensive heels clicking on the polished floor.

Chapter Fifteen

McQuede was hoping to have a moment to talk to Loris alone, but Ganner remained long after Preston had wandered off. He felt a twinge of annoyance as Ganner continued to occupy Loris' attention, talking about old times and events they had shared that excluded McQuede.

"Remember that Fourth of July when we all went out to Porter's Lake for a picnic?"

Loris' face lit for a moment. "That was Jerome's favorite spot, where he went to be alone, to write his songs. I'll never forget that day. We went canoeing, and Fredrick accidentally tipped the boat. I fell in the water, and if Jerome hadn't jumped in to save me . . ." Her voice trailed off, then stopped.

"We'll always miss him," Ganner said, touching her arm comfortingly.

"Once in a while I still go out to Porter's Lake," Loris said. "That old boathouse we all loved so much is about to fall in now."

"The Kenwells cite it as a hazard and want it demolished."

"Just like the old school," Loris added.

A new cluster of people had arrived. Preston returned, speaking to Loris in a low voice. "The Carlsons need your undivided attention. They've definitely brought their wallets, so let's take that pretty smile of yours over there. Don't forget to apply ample amounts of the old charm."

"Duty calls," Loris remarked, with an apologetic glance toward McQuede, as if she were reluctant to leave him. McQuede watched as Preston took her arm and guided her away. She worked so hard for the museum, her efforts tireless.

Ganner and he continued watching them until the well-dressed couple spirited Loris away, and she vanished into the corridor leading to her office.

Preston remained in the museum area. The moment he was alone, his ex-wife approached him. From the look on Preston's face, they were exchanging sharp, serious words. Then an elderly museum patron, no doubt a generous contributor, stepped forward with outstretched hands, causing Preston's frown to break into one of those ingratiating smiles he used on customers at the bank.

Once the elderly man was out of earshot, the argument started up again. This time McQuede could make out Heather's words. "I should have known I couldn't count on you to help me!"

She stormed away, leaving Preston looking as if he had been slapped in the face.

Heather had a very mean temper, McQuede noted. It

wouldn't be hard to imagine her getting even with the boy who had betrayed her or, for that matter, even breaking a bottle and stabbing Harlan in the throat.

"If you want my opinion, he's better off without that one," Ganner spoke up. "Why Fredrick still loves her is beyond me."

"Birds of a feather," McQuede suggested. "They're both very spoiled and willful. Handed all anyone could ever want without any effort. Like all that money Preston got for a graduation present. Isn't exactly fair, is it?"

"I don't know what his family showered on him, but all I got from my folks was a twenty-dollar watch." Ganner lifted his wrist as if still expecting to see some cheap dime-store brand with a plastic band instead of his nice silver Waltham.

"Of course, times were hard," he continued. "At least for my family. Those Prestons always stood for big money."

"In spite of the odds, you managed to make something of yourself," McQuede observed.

"I was determined not to end up working in the mine like my father, growing old and sick before my time."

"Where did you go to college?"

Ganner hesitated a moment, then replied, "Stanford University." As if gauging McQuede's thoughts, he explained, "Believe me, getting into the university of my choice was tough. Even working and with scholarships, it would have been impossible. My dad died in an accident at the coal mine, and the insurance policy paid for most of my tuition."

Hard to imagine that Ev Ganner had grown up on the same side of the tracks as Harlan Daniels and Jerome Slade. And yet he had managed to graduate from college, get a good job as school principal, and become a respected member of Black Mountain society, accepted by people like the cliquish Prestons.

Ganner stared across the room at Preston, who had returned to where members of the class of '88 were gathered. "Despite all that's happened, Fredrick is insisting on holding this reunion as scheduled," Ganner said. "The way he goes on about his 'glory days' sometimes turns my stomach. They can all be such hypocrites." He continued glaring at the small group. "You should have seen the way they treated me in high school, before I made good."

"I take it high school wasn't exactly the happiest time of your life."

"I'd just as soon forget all about it. I believe in living for the now."

"I've always been a today person myself," McQuede responded. He sort of liked Ganner, despite their competition over Loris. So many people wasted their present happiness by dwelling in the past, whereas men like Ganner left yesterday behind and concentrated on today. McQuede had to admire a man who had come up from nothing and managed to make a success of himself.

McQuede wanted to spend some time with Loris, but she flitted about the room from group to group like a colorful butterfly, and he didn't want to interfere with her work.

More pretentious than usual, Heather was frantically playing the room. She stood at the front entrance greeting the late arrivals. Something was bothering her tonight, enough to allow her to show her claws in public.

The moment the people stopped coming in, Heather intercepted Loris, just as she had Preston. McQuede could tell by Heather's indignation that if he didn't intercede, an ugly scene was going to break out. He excused himself and strode away from Ganner toward them, crossing the room just in time to hear Heather's cutting words.

"I knew Jerome was dead when he didn't meet me! No one in his right mind would choose you over me!"

McQuede increased his pace. He could tell by the way Loris drew herself up that she wasn't going to let this insult pass.

Heather turned on him with the same fury. "I told you not to go near my house again! You had no right going there this afternoon, upsetting my mother. I want you to stay away from her!"

Before McQuede could reply, Preston stepped to the center of the room, raffle box in hand, all pomp and circumstance. "Attention, folks. We need everyone to go into the auditorium. I am going to start the drawing now. The first is for the grand prize of five hundred dollars."

People clamored forward, packing the adjoining room. McQuede wanted to detain Loris and have a word with her, but she had followed Preston and stood beside him. McQuede edged over to the side.

Preston reached a hand into the box. "The winning ticket is Number 110."

Wasn't that his number? Or was it 112? McQuede never won anything. Probably he was mistaken. Nevertheless, he rummaged in his wallet for the ticket stub Loris had given him days ago.

"Where is number 110?"

Just what had happened to that ticket? McQuede was almost certain he had the winning number. Ah, yes, he found it. It had slipped into the lining of his wallet.

The moment his hand closed around his winning number, he felt a tug at his arm. "Could you read my ticket?" Bernie asked anxiously. "I didn't bring my glasses. Everything's just a big blur."

McQuede took the stub from Bernie.

Preston held up his hand. He joked, "Well, folks, it appears someone is reluctant to claim their five-hundred-dollar prize."

Bernie watched McQuede anxiously. The drawing seemed to mean so much to him. Five hundred dollars would be a fortune to the old man, who lived on a shoestring pension. McQuede looked at the two tickets, then handed one back to Bernie, saying, "Number 110. Looks like you're the lucky one, Bernie."

Bernie Slade's eyes lit in amazement, then with sheer joy, the kind McQuede had never before seen in anyone.

"Wait! That's me!" He waved the ticket triumphantly in the air. "That's my number! I've got the winning ticket!"

McQuede was aware of Loris heading toward him. She stopped a moment, looking in amazement from Bernie, who hurried forward to claim his prize, to McQuede, who was crumpling the remaining ticket stub into his pocket.

Loris reached his side, looking puzzled. "But I thought—wasn't your number—?"

McQuede understood that she had come over to congratulate him. A look of realization crossed her face. Loris gazed at him admiringly, then said in a very low voice, "You're definitely one of the good guys, Jeff McQuede."

McQuede was in high sprits. As the crowd began to clear, he started to search for Loris. He hadn't had a chance to talk to her alone all evening. He didn't see her anywhere and wondered if she might have gone back to her office. Maybe he could catch her there and make plans to see her this weekend.

The door to the office was slightly ajar. McQuede stopped abruptly and drew in a deep breath. A slow sense of shock stole over him, then a clenching around his heart that was almost physical. Now he knew why Loris hadn't contacted him all week. His rival was not a black-and-white picture of a long-dead boy, but the flesh and blood man who held Loris tightly in his arms—Ev Ganner!

Chapter Sixteen

Thoughts of Loris once again intruded into McQuede's duties. All day long he kept seeing her in Ganner's arms. He pushed aside the papers he was working on and leaned back in his desk chair. He had even considered stopping by the museum and out and out asking her for some explanation for her being in Ev Ganner's arms, but in the end, he decided against an open show of jealousy.

The phone rang.

"Jeff, it's Loris," she said hurriedly. "When I got home a while ago, I found my front door forced open! Someone has broken into my house, just like they did at the museum." She stopped, then said in anguish, "My priceless Carlo painting is gone."

"Stay there. I'll be right over."

As McQuede sped from his office to Black Mountain Pass, he thought of Sammy Ratone. Sammy knew the value of the Carlo work. Not long ago he'd tried to purchase the painting from Loris. That, along with the fact that he had arrived in town yesterday evening, made Sammy suspect number one. Whether he was guilty of this particular crime or not, similar incidents would be happening more and more frequently now that Ratone had a foothold—an office, so to speak—in Coal County.

By the time he reached the city limits, McQuede admitted to himself that he was assuming too much. Loris had mentioned her valuable painting in front of many people at yesterday's raffle.

Loris' pale, yellow house was set back from the street, half-hidden by trees. The approach of evening cast shadows across the yard, causing the high fountains and clusters of bushes to take on a sinister aspect, and offering places of concealment where someone could lurk unnoticed.

McQuede saw the same shadows altering Loris' face as she met him. She looked alone and vulnerable. McQuede fought an impulse to draw her close and comfort her, but images of Ganner interfered, making him maintain a professional distance.

McQuede examined the lock and concluded it had probably been the work of the same person who broke through the door at the museum. He strode past Loris and stopped, staring at the blank wall above the fireplace where Loris' cherished *Night Spirit* had hung.

"Is anything else missing?"

"All my jewelry is here, but wait, I need to check on another item." As she spoke, Loris released a small catch that opened a drawer of an oak desk. "My father gave me this gun years ago. I always keep it here." Tucked inside was a small .22 caliber revolver. "It's here. It's so easy to find, I wonder why he didn't take it. Guess he had his eye on my painting and wasn't interested in anything else."

"Do you have any idea who would do this?"

"No, but a lot of people knew about the Carlo."

"I'll have the house dusted for prints, but we're not likely to find any. I'll be frank with you, Loris. It's going to be next to impossible to get your painting back. I hope it was insured."

"Not for enough." Loris glanced at the empty space where the painting had hung. "Besides, I'll never be able to replace it. It was one of a kind."

Certainly, a valuable painting had been stolen, but the robber could have used this theft as a decoy to direct attention away from what he really wanted. After all, he had broken into the museum to steal a photo; photos had been stolen from Fenton's studio, and last night Loris had mentioned having pictures of the class of '88.

"I want you to check on something else. See if all of your photographs are here."

"I was just looking at them yesterday, trying to find some pictures for the reunion. They're in the basement."

McQuede went with her downstairs, where Loris opened an old humpbacked trunk. "This is where I put them." She whirled around, "Jeff, they're not here! They were only pictures of picnics and outings. Nothing anyone would want."

"You've heard about the break-in at Fenton's photo shop," he explained. "This might all be related to Jerome's death. The killer might be looking for incriminating evidence, a photo that might be a threat to him."

For a moment she looked frightened. "Whoever broke in here is the one who murdered Jerome, is that what you're saying?"

Once again McQuede felt a longing to hold her close

and tell her that everything would be all right. But remembering Ganner, he put aside this inclination and said officially, "It's very likely there's a connection."

They went back upstairs, where Loris sank down on the couch as if she was suddenly very tired. McQuede seated himself on the platform rocker facing her. He leaned forward, saying, "I need to ask you some questions, Loris. I understand you borrowed Howard Birk's truck."

"Why are you asking me about that?" she said coldly. "You act as if you're questioning one of your suspects."

"I'm just gathering information."

"I didn't even borrow the truck," Loris said with an edge of annoyance in her voice. "Ev told me I could have some of the school's old display cases for the museum, the ones that were slated to be destroyed. I was going to use it, but Ev offered to bring them over in his van."

Ev Ganner to the rescue—that figured.

"I've noticed the animosity between you and Heather Kenwell," McQuede continued. "It was over Jerome, wasn't it?"

"All this happened so long ago. Is it necessary to go over it?"

"I'm afraid it is."

"Jerome and I were thrown together when our English teacher asked me to tutor him."

Loris didn't go on, so McQuede prompted, "And you fell in love with him."

"I wasn't the only one in love. Jerome said I was his girl, and he wanted me forever."

McQuede knew the feeling. He waited.

"The night of the spring dance, Jerome told me he intended to meet Heather just as they had planned some time back. He told me he was going to tell her that he had changed his mind, that he wasn't taking her to Vegas with him." Loris' voice lost volume, became faraway, as if trying to break out of an encasement of memories. " 'I'm going to be a big star,' Jerome told me, 'then I'm returning to Black Mountain for you.' "

"And that's what you wanted?"

"I was deeply in love and I wanted to leave Black Mountain."

"And that's the last you heard from him."

"Yes. But he meant it, Jeff, I know he did. I couldn't believe it when months went by and he never contacted me. Of course, I had heard about how he'd used his father's credit cards and ended up in Vegas. I thought he might have gone from there to California. He'd talked about Los Angeles too, saying that was a place loaded with opportunities."

Trying to maintain his formal tone, McQuede asked, "Did you ever try to find out what became of him?"

"I made inquires, but they got nowhere. In the end, I had to accept that Jerome had forgotten all about me."

All while Loris had talked, she hadn't looked at McQuede. She didn't now. She wearily ran fingers through her thick, blond hair. When she spoke again, her words were distant, as if McQuede's aloofness had transferred itself to her. "So there's the story. Is that what you wanted to hear?"

"What do you think happened that night? Just between you and me."

"Heather happened."

Her words had a familiar ring, reminiscent of Fredrick Preston's.

"I'm convinced Heather knows what happened to Jerome," Loris stated emphatically. "Heather can't take rejection—you probably can see that for yourself. Jerome was going to tell Heather that he was leaving without her. I can't help thinking that she might have killed Jerome, not on purpose, but in one of those temper tantrums she's known to have."

"If she did, how does Harlan Daniels fit in?"

"Harlan supplied alcohol for her underage parties. She might have turned to him to help her cover it up. She could have given him Jerome's credit cards to use so no one would question Jerome's disappearance."

McQuede replied, "Killing Harlan in such a horrible way doesn't seem the work of a . . ." He was going to say *lady*, but changed his last word to "woman."

"Women can be more wrathful than men," Loris stated with certainty.

Chapter Seventeen

M_cQuede had stopped by the Black Mountain Police Department and asked the chief to send a patrol car past Loris' house for a few days. On the drive back to Durmont, McQuede swung into the Shady Lane Motel, where Sammy always stayed whenever he was in the area. Sammy might like luxury, but he liked Marty Stein, the motel's owner, more. And strangely, Marty, with her bold manner and dyed black hair, returned Sammy's affection.

McQuede didn't have to inquire at the desk, for he found a car with a Nevada tag parked at the end of the line of shoddy cabins. He knew Sammy would be in room 12, rather than 13, for Sammy feared the number 13 would be an omen that would heap misfortune upon him.

Too bad, McQuede thought, that he hadn't taken it.

He knocked loudly. After a while, a curtain parted. Then Sammy, in stocking feet, wearing tight jeans and a white undershirt that stretched across his fat stomach, opened the door.

"Ha!" Sammy said exuberantly, "You must be here to

welcome me on behalf of the local Chamber of Commerce. You're lucky to find me, pal." He winked. "I just got back from having a drink or two with Marty."

McQuede smelled beer and cigar smoke as he stepped past him into the room.

"Have you come with a speech? With flowers?"

"I should have come with a search warrant," McQuede returned dryly. "This afternoon someone broke into Loris Conner's house and stole that painting you liked so much, the one by Carlo Owatah."

Sammy walked over to the nightstand and lifted a key ring that lay beside his wallet. He tossed it to McQuede. "No need for a warrant. You're free to search my car." He made a sweeping gesture around the small, tacky room. "Search my belongings too, while you're at it."

Sammy wasn't fool enough to leave stolen goods anywhere near him. McQuede handed him back the key ring. "When did you get into town?"

"Late last night."

"Then you've been here all day. Doing what?"

"Closing a business deal with Preston, did that this morning. When I left there, I went out to Ruger's. After that, I lounged around here." He winked again. "Marty can tell you that."

"Then you don't have much of an alibi."

"I like the way you do business," Sammy said with gusto. "Ha!" He pointed a finger at McQuede. "The old you're-guilty-until-proven-innocent method."

McQuede retreated to the door. "You're here. You had the opportunity. I found out what I wanted to know."

"McQuede."

McQuede turned back to Sammy.

"Feel free to harass me anytime. I'm as clean as a baby just out of a bathtub."

Another late night, McQuede thought, as he pulled into his office parking space. His deputy returned about the same time with a bag of sandwiches he had bought at Mom and Pop's. He poured McQuede a stiff cup of coffee and dragged a chair up close to the desk.

"We questioned Loris Conner's neighbors," Sid told him, "and none of them saw anyone around her house, not even a car."

"What else could we expect? Whoever broke in would make sure their vehicle was safely hidden. What else did you find out?"

"Nothing about the robbery," Sid replied. "We did get back a fingerprint report on The Drifter. The killer had carefully wiped the glasses and the table area. We have a few clear fingerprints from behind the bar. Mostly Harlan Daniels'. But Ruger's were there too, and, strangely enough, Ev Ganner's."

McQuede chose a ham and swiss on rye and unwrapped it as he talked. "Ganner was in The Drifter before the place was dusted."

"Who let him in?"

"Someone who's still afraid of the high school principal." McQuede took a swig of hot coffee. "I stopped and talked to Sammy. He spent a short time at the bank and ended the afternoon with Marty. Not much of an alibi."

"I questioned Ruger," Sid stated.

"What did he tell you?"

"Nothing. He kept taunting me, you know, the way that devil does. Someday we're going to catch those two thugs, and I want to be present when that happens. Do you think it ever will?"

"We'll keep trying." McQuede bit into the extra pickle Mom always slipped into the to-go orders for the station, because she knew how fond he was of them. They ate a while in silence.

"The way it looks, Harlan Daniels had left the table and started back to the bar. The killer pushed over the glass and chair as he rose, grabbed the whiskey bottle, and went after him."

"Or it could have happened the other way around," Sid countered, placing his coffee mug on the desk. "What if instead of being attacked, Harlan Daniels was the attacker? Then Harlan would have been killed in self-defense."

McQuede thought of Sandy Kurtz back in Lost Pines. If Harlan were the aggressor, he and his killer must have gotten into a vicious fight that resulted in Harlan's death. Harlan's being the aggressor would certainly go along with what Sandy had told McQuede about him.

McQuede had trouble getting to sleep. He lay staring at the ceiling thinking of Loris. Every time his thoughts would drift away from her, he'd see pools of blood, on the bar, on the counter, streaming from a dead man's throat. He listened to the mantel clock in the front room chime eleven, then twelve. He had just fallen asleep when the phone beside his bed jangled, jarring him awake.

"Sheriff, you've got to meet me right away."

McQuede recognized Preston's voice, demanding as always, though minus his usual affectedness.

"Tonight? Why?"

"Something urgent has turned up. I must see you at once."

"Why don't you come on over here?"

"I can't risk that. We can't be seen together. You'll know why when I talk to you. I don't want you to involve anyone else in this, either. You must come alone."

"I'll meet you downtown then."

"No, not in town. Come out near Porter's Lake. I can slip over there from where I live without being seen."

McQuede hesitated.

"If you're not going to talk to me right away," Preston said, panic in his voice, "it will be too late!"

McQuede would be a fool to meet one of the suspects in such a lonely area.

"Please, Sheriff. You're the only one I can confide in." Preston seemed genuinely frightened, enough to plead with him. "You just can't let me down. I'll meet you at the boathouse in twenty minutes."

Preston sounded as if he had something very important to tell him. A foolish risk to take, but with the complicated case he had on his hands, McQuede knew he had to take the chance. "I'll be there."

Porter's Lake was located about seven miles into Black Mountain Canyon. McQuede hadn't been out there for years. Loris had mentioned this lake to him, saying this was where Jerome had gone to write his songs and to be alone. Not always alone, McQuede thought, for Loris had been there too, with him—in love with him.

His sense of isolation deepened as he sped along the blacktop and swung left on the canyon road. The peak of Black Mountain, the town's namesake, cast a jagged, black outline in the dark sky. The closer he got to the remote lake, the more wary he became. Caution stirred up recurring thoughts of conspiracy and the warning that he may be falling into a trap.

Another left turn sent him jiggling along a gravel road through a meadow. The small lake, surrounded by scraggly pinions, lay just ahead. He slowed his car for the slope, and once he reached the clearing below, he pulled to a stop beside the sagging remains of a boathouse that set close to the water. No cars were in sight.

Strange that McQuede would beat Preston to the lake. Unless the same person who had been following McQuede had been following him too and had waylaid him on his way here. What had Preston said? "If you're not going to talk to me right away, it might be too late"? What if it was?

Switching on his flashlight, McQuede got out. He let the beam fall across the still water, then lifted it to the faded sign, PORTER'S LAKE, painted in amateurish letters across the old building. He stopped all motion, hearing only the sound of frogs and the scurrying of small animals, then he moved forward and kicked open the boathouse door.

He stepped inside. The smell of moist earth subjugated the scents of water and pines. He played the flashlight around scatterings of trash left from picnics, and allowed it to settle on a burned-out fire from some time long past.

"McQuede!"

McQuede swung around. His hand moved swiftly to his gun, and he aimed it toward the man in the doorway.

Chapter Eighteen

McQuede held his flashlight in one hand, his revolver in the other, both locked on Preston. Preston stood frozen in place like some scared animal. With his ruffled hair and windblown jacket, he didn't look at all like the in-control banker.

"This lake is a little out of the way for a late-night chat," McQuede said.

"That's why I chose it. If anyone sees us together, it's all over."

"What's all over?" McQuede asked.

"Heather's entire future is at stake. She's turned to me for help, and I can't let her down."

Obviously their estrangement existed only when things were going well. "Tell me all about it."

The bright beam from McQuede's flashlight reflected in Preston's dark eyes. "Why don't you lower that thing? And you won't be needing to hold that gun on me either."

"If Heather's run up against some big trouble, why

145

didn't she contact me directly?" McQuede said, replacing his revolver in his holster.

"She'd be livid if she knew I was talking to you. I swore to her I'd handle everything myself."

"You're dealing with blackmail, aren't you?"

"Don't think for a minute that I'm going to let him get away with something like this," Preston said righteously.

Was this the same man, McQuede thought, who had bought off Jerome to eliminate his competition for Heather?

"If this leaks out," Preston continued, "it will not only ruin her campaign, but her whole life." For a while he seemed overwhelmed by the gravity of the situation. "Heather's always lived for public approval. She wouldn't be able to cope with a big scandal."

"Tell me exactly what's going on," McQuede said.

Preston ran a distraught hand through his hair. He looked as if he were facing the most important challenge of his life and feared that any move he made might be the wrong one. "Heather has trusted me with this important job. If everything goes south, I'm going to get the blame."

"On the other hand," McQuede replied optimistically, "if it doesn't, you're going to be her new hero."

That seemed to settle his indecisiveness, caused him to square his shoulders, and say, "This concerns those photos stolen from Bruce's studio. They contained pictures of Heather that simply can't be made public."

"I've already heard about them."

"How did you find out?"

"From Fenton."

"I don't know what that little freak told you, but I'll assure you, it's not the real story. Heather would never pose for pictures like those. Bruce took them on the sly, without her knowledge or consent." Preston groaned. "If only I'd known just how scummy he really was, I wouldn't have rushed in and bailed him out of jail."

"Did Heather supply any information about the blackmailer?"

"No. He had this raspy voice, that's all she said. He demanded that she leave five hundred thousand in a duffle bag."

"That's just for now. The blackmailer probably plans on getting future payments."

"Not this one," Preston said confidently. "He told her once he has the money safely in his hands, he will mail the photos back to her."

"Only a fool would believe that."

"She thinks this is the only chance she has!" Preston exclaimed. "If she doesn't follow his instructions, he'll send the pictures to some scandal rag, who'll be more than happy to distribute them all over Wyoming. Not only that, but he said he'll mail them to her political backers." Preston stepped closer as if to emphasize his words. "You can see why nothing must go wrong."

"I've worked with blackmailers before," McQuede replied. "There's no guarantee. Plans blow up right in your face. You need to realize that those photos are likely to surface no matter how much money you hand over. If it were me, I wouldn't pay him a cent."

"You wouldn't mind the humiliation, but you're not Heather. She wants to go through with this. Money's no problem. The Kenwells have funds they won't even miss and so do I."

"When and where is this to take place? Do you know yet?"

"I know. But I won't tell you unless you assure me this is strictly between the three of us, just Heather, you, and me."

"You have my word."

"I'm going to bring the cash tomorrow night at ten o'clock. We're to leave the money in the park that adjoins the Country Club. The blackmailer said to place the duffle bag under the third picnic table south of the tennis court."

"He's likely to make last minute changes in his plans. If he does, I'll need to know at once." McQuede stopped short. "This could be very dangerous. Are you certain you want to make the drop-off yourself?"

"Yes, but I need your help. Heather just wants to pay the blackmailer off and be done with it, but I called you so you can catch him."

The impossible, McQuede thought, was always left to him.

McQuede made his own road across a high meadow and parked the Honda he had borrowed from Sid—one black as night—in a thick cove of trees. He cut down a steep angle and, making certain he was as well hidden as the car, took up his post.

A full moon, bleak and cold, shone overhead, spreading bright rays across the park area below. The designated table was set close to a road that wound upward to the lodge. The Country Club closed on Monday night, so he could expect no interference, in the form of hindrance or help.

McQuede had gone over every possible scenario. He had calculated all possibilities to his advantage, even to the time it would take him to reach his car in the event of a chase. Preston's involvement set him at a distinct disadvantage. McQuede wasn't at all sure what the man would do in an emergency, and that made him nervous.

He drew his revolver, feeling more in control with it in his hand, and waited tensely. The time had arrived for Preston to deliver the money—where was he? A breeze stirred through the branches that encircled him and sent a chill through him. After a while his fingers that clenched the gun began to feel numb.

Below him, all was quiet. Moonlight fell across the cement tables and the tennis court. Time crept by, impossible to gauge.

Above the intermittent gusts of wind, he caught the distant sound of a car engine. The noise grew closer, and with it came descending headlights. Preston's Cadillac stopped near the table. Through the trees, McQuede strained to see the scene below him.

Preston got out, then reached back into the car for the gym bag. McQuede was aware only of motion, of Preston's bending down near the table, then rising again, empty-handed.

McQuede had told Preston to deliver the money and leave as quickly as possible, but Preston was not carrying out his instructions. He stood, tall and still, for what seemed an endless time. He kept looking around, and McQuede had to admit, there was an element of the heroic in his stance, as if challenging the blackmailer to appear and confront him.

Get in that car, fool, McQuede said to himself.

Preston stayed his ground for a long while. McQuede

let out his breath as he finally got back into the Cadillac. He watched the red taillights disappear over the rise. Preston was headed home now, so he would be safely out of harm's way.

McQuede knew his wait would now draw to a quick close. No one greedy enough to extract money in this fashion would leave five hundred thousand dollars unguarded for long.

Alert to every sight and sound, McQuede gripped his revolver tighter. A crackling noise, footsteps against underbrush, sounded from behind him. Ready to press the trigger, McQuede swung the gun around. Moonlight illuminated a familiar face.

"It's me," the man whispered. "Fredrick."

"I told you to go home."

Preston came forward to stand at McQuede's side, and he peered down the slope. "I want to be here when you arrest him."

The words were barely out of his mouth when car lights appeared. Like two huge eyes, drawing ever closer, they looked ominous. This wasn't the dark vehicle that had been following McQuede, but a pickup, one with a short bed, probably a Chevy, a very old one.

The man too seemed old as he walked slowly toward the park bench, bent down with painful slowness, and retrieved the bag. He wore a cap whose brim blocked the moonlight, so McQuede had no chance of recognizing him.

"Let's go!" Preston said, snaking a gun from his coat pocket. "Let's get him!"

McQuede placed a restraining hand on his arm. "This isn't the one we want," he said in a low, steady voice. "This is the 'gofer' man. We'll have to follow him. He'll be sure to lead us to the blackmailer."

"We can't do that! We can't let him get away!"

"Just put that gun away and let me handle this."

McQuede stayed a while longer, until the dark figure below got into his vehicle, then both Preston and he bounded toward Sid's Honda.

"I know a shortcut," McQuede said, backing the car around. "We can't risk following him directly. But we can intercept him before he gets to Black Mountain Pass."

Preston leaned tensely forward. "Where?"

"At that railroad intersection on County Road 231. Now, hang on."

"You'll have to beat the train," Preston said. "The night run leaves the mine at ten."

The rugged mountain road was badly eroded, laden with high spots and scatterings of rock. They sped along, wheels sliding in places or, alternately, hitting hard and causing smashing jolts.

"Do you have any idea who we're following?" McQuede asked.

"No," Preston said. He seemed distracted, as if intent on hearing what McQuede did not, the distant sound of a train whistle.

The old mountain road ended at a blacktop. McQuede stepped harder on the gas, confident they would reach the intersection before the pickup. He was wrong by a split second. He saw the truck pull to a stop. The train, sending out one final shrill warning, was fast approaching.

McQuede could hardly believe what happened next. The pickup spurted across the track minutes before the train.

McQuede slammed on his brakes to avoid colliding with the heavily laden flatcars.

Preston's curse rang out above the clanging of metal against rails. "He's got away! We've lost him!"

McQuede remained, clutching the wheel, as if hypnotized by the rattling, by the moving letters UNION PACIFIC flashing before his eyes. Quickly recovering, he put the car in reverse. Another road set a mile or so north. There was a chance they could still intercept him. McQuede drove at a frantic pace, past the continual stream of cars with their heaping loads of coal. After what seemed like an endless drive, he doubled back and reunited with County Road 231 to Black Mountain Pass.

The road, of course, was empty.

"I should have handled this myself," Preston moaned. "If I had, I'd have caught him. I'd have made him talk, made him tell me the name of the blackmailer. Now we've not only lost Heather's money, but we're left with absolutely no clues." He whirled toward McQuede. "You're the one who bungled this! I don't know why I trusted you!"

McQuede drove up and down the streets of Black Mountain Pass, but he caught no glimpse of the pickup. He searched until he grew weary. Preston had sunk into a surly silence.

"It's no use," Preston said as McQuede pressed on with his search. "Just take me back to my car."

McQuede was glad to be rid of him. He dropped him off at the Country Club where he'd hidden his Cadillac, and then, with a sense of defeat uncommon to him, McQuede headed back to Durmont. Once at home, he sank down on his couch and wondered where he'd gone wrong, what he should have done that he hadn't.

Early the next morning, after a wakeful night, Mc-Quede checked with the vehicle department. Not many trucks fitting the description he gave them were registered. He copied down some names, among them Wiley Clegg, the town's jack-of-all-trades handyman.

He pulled up to Clegg's little shack, not far from Bernie Slade's place. He drew in his breath when he saw the pickup parked to the side of it—this had to be the same truck he'd seen last night.

Clegg, a hand to his back, answered the door. He was a skinny fellow with a deeply lined face and gray hair that spewed out from an overgrown crew cut. "What can I do for you?" he asked in a friendly way. "You find the idiot who's writing insults on my advertising signs?"

McQuede smiled a little, recalling the JACKASS-OF-ALL-TRADES signs. If things kept going the way they were, he might be in line for one of those labels himself.

"Have you caught him or not?" the old man asked impatiently.

"We're still working on that."

"Then what brings you here?"

McQuede decided to make it sound as if it were a known fact. "You were out at the Country Club last night. I understand you picked up a duffel bag there."

"How do you know so much about my business?"

"I was behind you when you reached the intersection of County Road 23l. You took quite a chance raring across the tracks in front of that train. Why did you do it? I want you to tell me that."

"You surely didn't come here to give me a ticket. I didn't harm anyone. It was getting late. You know how long those trains are. I didn't want to wait for a hundred cars to rattle by."

"Who hired you to go after that duffle?"

"A man asked me to fetch a bag for him, that's all I can tell you. His name's Ben Owen, if that's what you want to know. He gave me a fifty." Clegg's sudden laugh seemed too young and happy to spring from such a world-weary face. "Pretty good money for a twelve-mile drive, wouldn't you say?"

"You made this deal with Owen personally?"

"Nope. He called me."

"What did he sound like?"

"Kind of choked up and hoarse."

Raspy would be a more accurate word, McQuede thought, remembering the call he had gotten in Las Vegas.

"He must have had a bad cold. It got darn chilly last night. He probably wanted to stay in where it's warm."

"What was in the bag? Do you have any idea?"

"I didn't look. I suppose it was gym shoes and the like. He told me he'd been checking out the Country Club and stopped to play tennis with his wife. He forgot and left his duffel bag there. He'd seen one of my signs and wondered if I'd pick it up and bring it into town for him."

"But you didn't know him before this?"

"Nope. He's new in town. Leased that real fancy house out toward the Kenwells, on Twenty-eighth Street."

"That place has been vacant for a long while," McQuede said. "I always thought the Baxters intended to come back. Is that where you dropped off the bag?"

"Yeah."

"And he handed you your payment? What did he look like? This is very important. I must get an accurate description of him."

McQuede waited anxiously, thinking the blackmailer couldn't be anyone local or Clegg would know him, wondering if the description would in any way fit Sammy Ratone's or Ruger's.

"Can't do that," Clegg replied. "He left an envelope in the door with my fifty in it. I just opened the screen, laid down the bag, and left." He gave another of his free-spirited laughs. "Easy money, huh?"

McQuede believed him. Clegg had always eked out his bare living on the right side of the law. Everyone around here knew him and liked him. He was always on hand, ready and willing to perform the chores they didn't want to do themselves. "Thanks," McQuede said.

"I didn't do nothin' wrong, did I?"

"No."

Once back in his car, McQuede called Sid Carlisle. "I want you to phone David Baxter. You know him; he works for the Union Pacific over at Paxton. I want to know if he's rented his place to anyone."

"Will do."

McQuede stopped in front of the sprawling house, all rock and glass, modern in every sense of the word. The FOR RENT sign had been pulled up and lay facedown in the yard. He knew even before Sid returned his call what the answer would be.

"It's still vacant. It's not for sale, but they would rent it if the right people were to come along."

McQuede stared at the house. Heather being black-mailed so soon after the theft of Loris' expensive painting seemed an uncanny coincidence. If all these crimes were related, whoever had duped Clegg into doing his dirty work had not only gotten away with two murders, but now possessed Loris' painting and five hundred thousand in cash.

McQuede leaned tiredly against the steering wheel of the squad car. And where did that leave him? With zilch, zero. As much as he hated to admit it, he had been outfoxed.

Chapter Nineteen

Discouragement prompted McQuede to stop at Mom and Pop's Café early the next morning. His spirits always lifted after a stack of hotcakes and a cup or two of coffee, both mixed with heaping amounts of Mom's comforting words.

As he was finishing the last of his breakfast, Ev Ganner, looking as gloomy as McQuede felt, crossed to the counter and seated himself beside McQuede. Mom could always read moods; she began to divide her sympathy between them.

"You boys, you come in here with such long faces. Tell me, Ev, what's so bad that you've lost your smile?"

"My love life," Ganner promptly replied.

Mom placed a steaming mug of her strong brew in front of him. "I'm the right person to talk to: senior editor for the lovelorn."

"It's Loris Conner." Ganner cast McQuede a disheartened glance, one of rejection sprinkled with a shred of

157

hope. "I'll let you in on a little secret, Mom. I proposed to her the night they held that raffle at the museum. She flat turned me down."

The grayness that had encircled McQuede since the blackmailer's success immediately floated away. He'd almost walked in on the scene Ganner was talking about and had misinterpreted Loris' being held in Ganner's arms. She had never even been interested in Ev Ganner. McQuede wondered if she were thinking of someone else at the time—possibly of him.

"If you're harboring any illusions," Ganner said to McQuede, "you might as well forget them. She'll turn you down as fast as she did me."

"Don't tell me you two are rivals! This does have an unusual twist. Black Mountain's distinguished high school principal and the famous Coal County sheriff doing battle for the lady fair. Let me tell you what you obviously don't know. Loris is a career woman. She loves her lifestyle same as you love yours. Why would she want to change it? Why does she need the likes of either of you?"

"You're downright heartless," McQuede said.

Mom laughed.

Ganner took a deep swig of coffee. "And we walk through those doors for words of encouragement."

"Fate rules the world," Mom stated, "and you have to go along with it. May I quote Omar Khayyam, 'The Moving Finger writes; and having writ, moves on.' "

"I don't even know what that means," Ganner said.

"What *is* is the way it is," Mom explained, "so live with it."

"Don't know whether I can do that or not," McQuede replied with a chuckle. "That's an awful lot of *is*'s." Mc-Quede finished his coffee and set down the mug. "Here's my take. We're all faced with events we can't control. How we react to them is what makes our fate."

"Say you're faced with some terrible, crushing event," Mom cut in. "You can smile all you want, but you're never going to make it anything but what it *is*."

"Not another *is*," McQuede groaned.

"I agree with Mom," Ganner said. "Fate rules us all. All we can hope for is to accept it with some degree of graciousness."

"I disagree, and I can give you an example from your own life," McQuede responded, swinging around on the stool to face Ganner. "When your father was awarded that big settlement from Preston Coal, you could have run through the money, gambled it, tossed it away on women and cars. Instead, you used it to attend a prestigious university. And that made you what you are today."

"That was a terrible accident," Mom consoled, looking sober now. "I remember it. But I didn't know your dad was killed at the mine."

Ganner drank the last of his coffee. "You two are only adding to my pain," he said. He rose, laying a bill beside his cup. "I'll just take it elsewhere."

Ganner reached the door, where he turned back, his broad face lighting with a smile. "This old football player doesn't give up that easily. I'm going to make another run at the goal line."

"Don't let him beat you there," Mom advised McQuede after Ganner left.

What McQuede had found out from Ganner, along with Mom's cheering him on, prompted him to go from the café directly to the museum. He didn't know what he was going to do once he got there. Maybe he'd just toss his name into the hat, tell Loris he had fallen in love with her. He might even ask her to marry him too.

Because it was early morning, the place was empty of visitors. The bell jangled as McQuede opened the door, face to face with the ferocious stuffed bear that guarded the entrance. The animal had riled against his fate, snarling and snapping, ready to do battle—his feelings captured forever by those who passed this way. And look what had happened to him. Maybe Mom was right: acceptance *was* the key.

McQuede's footsteps sounded hollow on the wooden floor as he made his way back to Loris' office. He felt gripped by confusion. In his mind, he kept seeing her in Ganner's arms, in Jerome's arms, in everyone's arms but his.

McQuede stopped in the hallway. Loris' low voice drifted out to him, encircling him like some sort of warning, yet, at the same time, sounding sweet and sincere. She was singing an old love song. McQuede didn't recall this particular tune, although he ran through the songs he remembered from the late '80s. Her singing was a little off-key, but beautiful, at least to his ears.

"I could go on, but not this time . . . but not this time."

The sad lyrics, about being disappointed in love, sounded as if they had surfaced from some cruel past. The next refrain, "I could just let you go, but not this time . . . but not this time," made McQuede more discouraged than ever. It prompted him to think of Jerome, to picture him writing those poignant lines as he sat beside Loris at Porter's Lake.

Loris had been hurt deeply by Jerome, and the discovery of his death had caused an eruption of pent-up emotion, of love or pain or resentment, whatever it was. McQuede waited until the last strain faded away before making his presence known.

"I didn't know you could sing," he said, drawing forward from the doorway.

Loris looked embarrassed, as if he had caught her in some illegal activity. He stared at her solemnly. He knew, at that moment, that his rival had never been Ganner. Here loomed the event Mom had talked about, that no one could change no matter what he did or didn't do. Loris was never going to stop loving Jerome, was never going to let him go and love again.

"What do you want, Jeff?"

What he wanted was to crush her against him, to demand that she live in the real world, where hopes are dashed and loved ones die. He wanted to confess his feelings for her. Yet he stood severely straight, looking at her as if he had never seen her before, totally unable to reply.

"What did you want, Jeff?" she asked again.

Once more he hesitated. "To see when you want to have dinner with me," he managed to say.

"I have a very busy schedule right now, Jeff. Could I take a rain check?"

At least that wasn't a flat turndown.

Back in his office, McQuede lifted the paperweight from his desk, tipping it back and forth. The events starting with Jerome's death seemed to follow no discernable pattern, as strange and unrelated as the shifting flow of multicolored sand.

"You got mail," Sid said, crossing the room and placing a large, brown envelope in front of him. "See, it says *personal*."

McQuede glanced at the typed label, SHERIFF JEFF MC-QUEDE, no return address. He opened the envelope carefully, so as not to disturb fingerprints, dreading what he would find inside. He thought first of Heather's black-mailer, who now had both the photos and the money. Would this be some taunt? Had he sent copies of the photos of Heather to flaunt the fact that McQuede had failed to apprehend him?

If so, this delivery would be just one of many. Despite all the cash he got, the blackmailer was sending out the photos anyway, relishing the fact that he was ruining Heather Kenwell and her chance to win the election.

McQuede had guessed right: a picture was inside, a single black and white photo. But it wasn't what he expected. Two young people, dressed in evening clothes, were locked in tight embrace, lips meeting in a passionate kiss. He recognized the dark hair and handsome profile of Jerome, and then, with a jolt, the girl he held tightly in his arms, Loris Conner!

This photo must have been among those that Bruce Fenton had claimed were stolen from his studio. It had, without doubt, been taken at the Spring Fling Dance, for McQuede recognized the gown Loris had worn that night from the picture Fenton had shown him at his office at the old high school. What he didn't know was why it had been mailed to him.

Sid, peering over his shoulder, voiced McQuede's own thoughts. "Why would anyone send this to you? It doesn't incriminate anyone, unless being young and in love is a crime."

McQuede asked, more to himself than to Sid, "Do you think someone actually did steal photos from Fenton's studio, or do you believe Fenton sent this to me himself?"

"Why would Fenton chase you around with a pipe if he wasn't furious about being robbed?"

"To stop me from snooping. Remember, Fenton was at the high school the day that scoreboard light fell on top of me. He could have pushed it over the ledge, intending to end my investigation once and for all."

"And he sent this, why?"

"So I would be thinking of a suspect other than Heather."

"That sounds likely, but it's not the only possibility," Sid remarked. "What if the killer knew he'd find a picture in Fenton's studio that would link him with Jerome Slade's murder? This one was among those he stole. Now he's making use of it to throw you off the track."

"You're assuming this was one of the photos stolen from Fenton, but it could have belonged to someone else. Heather, for instance, to throw suspicion on Loris."

Or Preston, McQuede thought. Obviously Preston still loved Heather. He wanted Heather to see him as her hero and protector so he could win her back. "Or this could have been sent by Preston to keep us from focusing on Heather."

Sid gazed down at the picture. "Maybe someone's trying to tell us something, point us in the right direction. This Loris Conner might have killed Jerome Slade. The rejected lover, that's always a motive."

Did Loris know more about Jerome's murder than she was telling him? Or had Loris sent this to him herself as she sank deeper and deeper into a quagmire of grief . . . or guilt?

McQuede put the picture aside, wishing it would just go away, but the image of Jerome and Loris remained imprinted on his brain. He lifted it again, a thousand different emotions spinning through his mind. He was jealous of the picture and afraid of it too, as if it might tell him things he didn't really want to know, secrets laid bare in black and white.

Chapter Twenty

McQuede lost no time driving to Bruce Fenton's studio. The photographer shrank away as McQuede entered, as if fearing McQuede had come either to haul him off to jail again or to seek some personal vengeance for the attack on him.

Today Fenton seemed about as dangerous as a mouse. It was difficult to imagine this subdued, reclusive man was the same one who, with a mad gleam in his eyes, had viciously struck McQuede in the alley with a pipe.

McQuede placed the photograph on the countertop between them. "This one of yours?"

Fenton pushed at his glasses, peered at the photo, and shrank even further away, saying in a toneless voice, "Yes. I took that at the spring dance."

The thought of Fenton lurking in the shadows, sneaking a picture of a stolen kiss between two young lovers renewed McQuede's sense of disgust.

"Do you have any idea how it ended up on my desk this morning?"

Fenton's eyes widened in alarm. "I didn't send it, if that's what you think. I don't even have a copy of it anymore. It was among those stolen from my studio."

He faltered, all color draining from his face and, with a horrified gasp, he asked, "Did you receive any other pictures?"

"No," McQuede replied shortly, not going on, not adding that it would be only a matter of time before the risqué shots of Heather started turning up as well.

After a silence in which McQuede stared with suspicion at Fenton, he demanded, "Do you know why anyone would have sent this to me?"

Fenton frantically shook his head. In the dim light his lank strands of hair looked even more straggly, more shot with gray.

"Are you sure no one besides the robber has a copy of this photo?"

Fenton didn't answer at once, then blurted out, "Loris." He went on hurriedly, "She was interested in photography, too. We worked together on the junior and senior annuals."

McQuede tapped the picture. "You surely didn't plan to put that in the high school yearbook. What made you take this picture?"

Once more he shrank away. "You think I'm some sort of freak, don't you?"

McQuede made no reply.

After a few moments Fenton composed himself, stepped closer, and stared down at his work. "I'm an artist. This is living, breathing art. I wandered around the night of the dance snapping random shots, and there they were." His voice became faraway, almost dreamy. "So beautiful. I saw before my eyes the essence of my craft—true emotion. They both looked at me when the flash went off, but they didn't object."

"So you were just roaming around taking pictures," McQuede said, but he decided that what he was really doing was stalking girls, the same way he did Heather.

Fenton looked fondly down at his photo. His love for photography made him verbal, almost eloquent. "Good photographs aren't just replicas of reality. They are open doors to the meaning of life—to feelings. I have succeeded in capturing a moment in time, one that can't grow old, can't change, one that doesn't lie—like people do. Here it is, before you. Young love in all its glory."

"But all you do with them is file them away in some cabinet."

Fenton took McQuede's words as the ultimate insult. "I have used these as practice runs for some of my best work. You're like all the rest. You think I'm nobody, but I have displayed in many important shows all around the state."

"Why did you give this photo to Loris? Did she ask you for it?"

"After Jerome left, I gave her lots of photos, of picnics, of dances. I am the eyes of Black Mountain. I know more than other people do. I knew how she felt about him." Fenton glanced down at the image of the two young lovers he had captured so long ago. "Loris told me she'd always treasure this photo."

McQuede scooped up the picture, and abruptly left the studio, deciding to return to the museum.

Loris was engrossed in her work, arranging a new display in one of the Arapaho cases.

"You ever see this before?" McQuede asked.

Loris turned toward him, startled, then she set down the box of arrowheads she'd been arranging into patterns and stepped closer. "Yes. Bruce gave me a copy."

"And you kept it where? Among those school pictures you claimed were stolen?"

Loris didn't answer his question. When she spoke again, her voice, in fact, her whole attitude, had taken distance. "How did you get this?"

"Through an anonymous sender. I thought you might be able to tell me who."

"How would I know?"

McQuede detected a coolness in her voice he'd never heard before. She did know something vital. "Just what is going on, Loris? I'd like to know."

"I have a theory I'm working on."

McQuede knew it would involve Heather Kenwell and the fact that she had in some way caused Jerome's death or had killed him herself. "It would be a mistake for you to keep any information from me."

"I think so too," Loris replied. "But I can't tell you anything now. I need to talk to Bruce first. If this turns out to be of any importance, I'll let you know."

"I can't let you investigate on your own. Don't you understand that whoever killed Jerome and Harlan is cold-blooded to the core?"

"Don't worry," Loris replied. "I'm not in any danger."

She sounded certain. So did her refusal to share what she was planning to do. McQuede wondered, as his gaze held hers, how deeply involved she was in all of these happenings. Whether he wanted to acknowledge it or not, he might be dealing with not a victim, but a suspect.

Back at his office, McQuede felt sorry that he hadn't stayed longer at the museum, that he hadn't demanded that Loris tell him everything she knew or believed. At the same time, he felt a strange sinking in his heart. He knew he had to analyze this case as a lawman with years of experience behind him, and not let his thoughts and decisions be distorted by his feelings.

First off, it was possible that Loris had shown up after the dance before Heather had arrived. Jerome might have told her he had changed his mind and was taking Heather with him to Vegas—astounding news, betraying news, that a young girl crazy in love wouldn't handle well. A love triangle, a fight, an accidental death.

McQuede had seen how the discovery of Jerome's remains had deeply distressed Loris, as if it had forced deeply buried memories to surface—like the skull that Birk's backhoe had exposed.

Had Jerome scorned Loris, like Harlan had Sandy Kurtz? He did not believe Loris was capable of murder, but what about the passionate teenager she had once been?

McQuede found himself thinking of Sandy Kurtz, of the pain and vindictiveness in her eyes that time had done nothing to diminish. At what point does hurt turn to rage? Is murder ever justified?

McQuede's thoughts continued along this line almost against his will: the idea that Jerome's death had sprung from a fight between Loris and the boy who had betrayed her. McQuede cringed at the vision of Loris lifting some weapon and crushing Jerome's skull.

If Loris had been to blame for his death, it had been a result of a moment's bitter rage. Afterward, Loris would have been beside herself with fear. Enough to have enlisted the help of Harlan, the town ruffian, on the night of the dance. Harlan wouldn't have known Slade had been murdered, not until the day the high school was demolished. He would have believed Jerome had given Loris the credit cards to mislead his father and the law, so they couldn't trace him to wherever he'd actually gone. When McQuede found out Harlan had made a paper trail, Harlan might have told Loris he wasn't sharing the blame and was going to the police.

In his wildest imagination, McQuede couldn't believe that Loris had planned these crimes. Both of these murders would have had to have been impulsive, in some way unavoidable. Harlan, a brutal thug, intended to protect himself to the end. When Loris had come to talk to him, he might have become angry enough to attack her, as Sid suggested, and she might have killed him in self-defense.

A big part of McQuede rejected all of these thoughts. Loris wasn't guilty of anything. She was the perfect woman, *his* perfect woman, not capable of committing hideous crimes. Or was he seeing in black and white because he was in love with her? For the first time, McQuede wondered if he really wanted to find out what had happened to Jerome Slade.

Chapter Twenty-one

Ev Ganner pushed his way into McQuede's office. "We don't have a second to spare!" he shouted. He strode deeper into the room frantically waving a sheet of paper. "I found this note in my e-mail!"

As Ganner drew closer, McQuede noted the sweat on his forehead and the way his hands shook as he thrust the paper toward him.

Ganner's voice became choked. "I can't believe it! It looks as if Loris . . ."

McQuede scanned the brief message.

Ev,
A long time ago, I did something horrible. The past can't be buried. It's always kept pace with me, surfacing to ruin everything in my life. It's kept me from loving you or anyone else. Days ago, I committed an even worse crime. I can't live with it any longer. Please forgive me.

Loris

"She's going to kill herself!" Ganner cried out with anguish. "We've got to stop her!" Ganner didn't wait for McQuede to answer. He whirled to the door. "I'm going to find her!"

Tire wheels skidded as Ganner pulled out onto the road. Then silence engulfed McQuede, a kind of silence he had never before known.

Loris' car wasn't in its usual spot in the museum's parking lot. The doors being locked during museum hours renewed McQuede's desperation. No chance existed that she would be inside. Still he called Sid, told him to get keys to the museum, and do a search. "But first off, put out an APB on Loris Conner."

"What's going on?"

"I saw a suicide note."

"Is it for real?" Sid asked. "Or something someone forced her to write?"

"No way of telling."

Even though Ganner had probably just checked Loris' house, McQuede headed there next. He deliberately slowed his speed, hoping it would clear his head and help him think.

Loris' car was missing. A heavy shoulder, doubtlessly Ganner's, had smashed through the door, causing the lock to hang askew. McQuede did a quick search, which ended at the desk in the front room. He stared down at the computer where the note had been written, but decided he wouldn't take time to turn it on. Next, he clicked the catch, as he'd seen Loris do and opened the left-hand drawer. Just as he feared, her .22 revolver was gone.

Tortured thoughts ran through McQuede's mind. If only Loris could hold on until he could find her.

With growing desperation, McQuede pulled up to the ruins of the demolished school and leaped from the squad car. In the south corner, a triangular wall of the old gymnasium still stood—the perfect place for a suicide. Broken stone crunched under McQuede's feet as he raced toward it. He tried to drive away the image of Loris' crumpled form, blood pooling from a single bullet wound to the heart.

McQuede had to force himself to step around the rise of rock and cement and gaze down at the rubble behind it. No sign of Loris. He slowly let out his breath.

His relief was short lived. Just because the catastrophe he'd prepared himself for hadn't taken place here, it didn't mean she was safe.

When McQuede had talked to Loris last, she had mentioned her plan to check out some theory with Fenton. In case she had discussed some crucial idea with him, McQuede decided to stop by his studio.

Fenton backed away as McQuede entered. "Has Loris been here?"

Fenton hugged his arms to his sides as if McQuede had ushered in a chill wind. He must have just arrived at the studio, for he still wore a faded green jacket. He peered at McQuede. His glasses, which looked out of alignment, caused his thin features to appear strange and distorted.

"I know you've seen her!" As McQuede spoke, he crossed the room, his gaze falling to a large photograph that lay alone on the edge of the counter. As he reached for it, Fenton tensed, as if he were on the verge of one of his unpredictable mood swings. "What's this?"

"An enlargement I made for Loris."

The shot had been taken at night. Like the majority of

Fenton's photos, the focus was on Heather. The atmos-
phere, the sharp contrasts of light and dark, gave it an eerie
quality, like one of Carlo Owatah's paintings. It evoked feelings of slipping into some secret world of half-forgotten
memories or dreams.

Heather, shoulder-length hair fanning behind her in the
breeze, looked on the verge of tears. He knew this had
been taken the night of the dance, although Heather wasn't
wearing an evening gown, just jeans and a heavy coat.

He was aware of Fenton's long fingers tapping an anxious drumbeat on the countertop. He looked keyed up, as
if at any moment he was going to erupt into some violent
action.

"Loris must have found the old school pictures you
gave her that she thought had been stolen. This picture
was taken the night Jerome died, isn't that right?"

"Yes. That night . . . ," Fenton faltered, then went on,
his voice high-pitched and nervous, "I hung around after
the dance, thinking this might be the last photo I would
ever take of her."

McQuede knew he held in his hand the key to the crime.
He studied the picture again, trying to see what Loris had
seen. The wall of the new gymnasium rose just behind
Heather. A huge truck was parked on the street beyond the
new building, one with the lettering of Birk's construction
company. McQuede could barely discern the front of another vehicle, one half-concealed by the frame of the high
school. This one wasn't a truck, but a much smaller vehicle with an unusual, rounded top.

If Loris thought she might find evidence in this photo
that Heather had killed Jerome, McQuede didn't see it.

Heather's clothes showed no traces of Jerome's blood, no rips from a struggle, no dirt from having just buried him. She did hold some object in her hand. "What is this? Do you know?"

Fenton replied, "I remember. She was holding a large bag, the kind the kids all carried then. That's just the handle showing there."

"Did you see Jerome that night?"

"No."

McQuede scanned the photo again, taking note of every detail. He looked again at the vehicles. The suspicions that had been lurking in the back of his mind suddenly surfaced, filling him with a sense of horror. In an instant, what had happened the night of that spring dance became amazingly clear.

"Where are you going?" Fenton's hollow words followed him as he half ran toward the squad car.

When McQuede had left the office, he'd planned to check every place he could think of that was in any way linked with Jerome. Porter's Lake, where the boy had gone to write his songs and to be with Loris, was next on his list.

McQuede's siren screamed and the blue and red lights flashed as he barreled down the isolated blacktop, cursing the distance to the remote lake. His tires kicked up loose dirt as he swung left onto the rutted canyon road. Black Mountain, like an omen, loomed above him, casting dark shadows.

The car jogged along the eroded road, but he didn't slacken the speed. Ahead of him through the shield of trees he could see the dilapidated boathouse. The late afternoon sun reflected on the glassy surface of the lake.

Even though he didn't see Loris' car, he bounded out, throwing open the door to the boathouse, dreading what he might find.

Loris, arms and legs bound, lay on her back on the cement floor, her eyes closed. McQuede, horrified, drew to a halt. Then he approached her and knelt beside her. He was grateful to see the rise and fall of her breath.

She looked at him, dazed for a moment, then with disbelief. "Jeff, it's you!"

McQuede quickly untied her and drew her close to him. "Thank God I've found you." He held her tightly for a moment, and then released her. "We must hurry. The killer will be back. He plans to make your death look like a suicide."

"I had just left the studio. I was on my way to see you," Loris said in a shaken voice. "I was just getting into my car when he struck me from behind. When I woke up, I was out here. I didn't see him, but I know who he is!"

McQuede half-lifted her to her feet. "He may be out there now."

"I was so wrong about everything," she gasped. She took a deep, sobbing breath. "I thought all the time the killer was Heather. But *he* was out there, too. How could I have been so stupid? I went right to him with the photo. Bruce . . ."

As if his name had caused him to materialize, Fenton appeared at the doorway. His eyes behind the round glasses glittered like cut glass. They gleamed irrationally, as if he were out of touch with reality, the way they had the night he had struck McQuede with the pipe. His startled gaze shifted from McQuede to Loris.

"You're not Heather," he said.

His words made no sense to McQuede. He wondered if

they did to Fenton himself, or if, because of a lifetime of obsession, he had slipped into a world of his own.

"I thought Heather had found out you were after her," Fenton said to McQuede. "I thought she'd be hiding out here. That's why . . ." He looked around, seeming to be in a state of total confusion. "Where is Heather?"

Fenton was used to stalking Heather; he had years of practice. That's how he had been able to follow McQuede from the studio to the lake without being spotted.

"When you looked at that photo, I knew exactly what you thought. The same thing Loris did. But it's not true. I can't let Heather take the blame, when I know the truth."

"You killed him," Loris moaned. "So Heather wouldn't leave Black Mountain, and you could always be around her."

"She's innocent. Heather didn't kill anyone. I know. I was there . . . I—"

At that moment, a gun blast sounded. Loris screamed. Fenton's eyes widened. He groaned and staggered forward. He hit the floor before McQuede could reach him. McQuede shifted his gaze from Fenton to the man who stood in the doorway, a revolver in his hand.

"Good thing I got here in time!" Ganner exclaimed. His exaltation immediately diminished as he stared down at Fenton. "Poor Bruce," he said, aghast. "I always knew he walked a thin line, that someday he'd snap. He was going to kill you both." Ev Ganner lowered the gun. "Loris, are you all right?"

"Yes. He didn't harm me."

Ganner watched as McQuede bent over Fenton, checking for a pulse.

"Is he . . . ?" Ganner stepped forward, his face pale in the waning light.

McQuede looked up at him. "He's dead."

"Oh, no," Loris cried.

"It's for the best, Loris. Bruce wouldn't have been able to handle spending the rest of his life in prison." Ganner glanced down at Fenton's body, at the tangled, graying hair and the blood that spread across his faded green jacket.

"I had to shoot him," Ganner told McQuede. "I couldn't take the chance, not with Loris' life. He's armed, isn't he?"

"Yes," McQuede said, rising. "Your action was clearly justified."

"What do we do now?"

"I'll go to the squad car and call for help."

McQuede thought of Loris' broken door, of the strength of the person who had thrown his shoulder against it. Ganner would be a match for him. McQuede had to depend solely on the element of surprise. Once behind Ganner, he whirled back, grabbing his elbow and wrist. He wrenched the gun from Ganner's hand. At the same time, he reached for the handcuffs and snapped them around Ganner's wrists.

"What? What are you doing?" Ganner gasped. He attempted to fight back, but the speed of McQuede's attack had rendered that impossible.

"What's going on?" Loris cried. "I don't understand."

McQuede spoke in a low, steady tone. "Ev Ganner, you're under arrest for the murder of Jerome Slade and Harlan Daniels. You have the right to remain silent . . ."

Chapter Twenty-two

McQuede's deputy arrived quickly in response to his call, and Loris rode back to town with him. Shortly afterward, an ambulance arrived to take away Bruce Fenton. That left McQuede to transport Ev Ganner back to the station.

McQuede knew who had committed these crimes when he saw the photo in Fenton's studio. He had remembered the talk on the night of the raffle about the cars the kids had driven in high school. That's why he recognized the distinctive shape of Ganner's Volkswagen. Even though Ganner had clearly stated that he'd been home by 11:00, he had in fact still been at the school. His car was parked at the crime scene when Heather had arrived to meet Jerome. "You remained at the school long after the others had left. You didn't realize it, but Fenton caught your lie on camera."

That picture, which linked him to Jerome's death, was what Ganner had been after. He broke into Fenton's studio looking for it and into Loris' house—covering up his tracks by stealing the Carlo painting and by blackmailing

179

Heather. But he didn't find the photo he wanted, the one with his Volkswagen in it, because Loris had removed it and taken it down to Fenton's studio to be enlarged.

"Overkill, that was your mistake," McQuede said. "You shouldn't have stolen that class picture from the museum. It only called attention to Jerome Slade's disappearance."

"That fool Fenton shouldn't have brought it to the museum in the first place," Ganner said. "I didn't want it hanging there as a reminder, so everyone that passed by would talk about him and why he never graduated."

"That's why you were so opposed to the demolition of the school. You were afraid Jerome's remains would be found."

"Once the committee had made up its mind, it was out of my hands. All I could do was prepare in case the bones did turn up."

Ironically, McQuede thought, Ganner had been on hand when Jerome's body was found. He had no choice but to identify that ring of Jerome's or risk throwing suspicion on himself.

Many clues existed that pointed to Ganner. He had been present the day of McQuede's accident at the school. He had known Loris had asked to borrow Birk's black pickup, so he took it himself, hoping to use it in his plans to stop McQuede's investigation.

"I thought it was strange that Mom didn't remember your dad having an accident at the mine," said McQuede. "That's because it never happened. I got to thinking about that later, and realized you were lying, that you had never received a settlement from Preston Coal. That's why you killed Jerome Slade—for the graduation gift, the one

Preston handed over to Jerome so he would leave Black Mountain without Heather."

"I've always been a decent person," Ganner said, gazing forlornly from the window of the fast-moving vehicle.

McQuede cast him a sideways glance, thinking how much he sounded like Sammy Ratone.

"I never once went along with Harlan and Jerome on those robberies. I wanted better for myself." His voice took on an edge of anger. "Then when graduation drew near, everyone was going off to college. They had a bright future, Preston at the bank, Loris at the museum, and there I was with no prospects but work at the coal mine."

He fell silent, then said vindictively, "It wasn't fair, all that money Preston handed to Jerome. Jerome was a born loser! What would he have done with that big stake? He was going to fritter it away on some hopeless shot at fame. I used it to go to the university. I made something of myself. Look at all these years I've spent helping kids, being a role model, an asset to the community. I came back here because I wanted everyone to see that Ev Ganner, who they shunned and looked down on, was a success!"

"And you believe that what these people think of you is worth murder?"

"That's not the only reason," Ganner said disdainfully, "I saw Jerome accept that bribe money from Fredrick. I was so angry! He was going to ditch Heather and use the money to run off with Loris." Indignation filled his voice. "What kind of person would do that?" He paused, groping for words. "Still, I didn't mean to kill him. I just hit him too hard."

"Then you buried him, took his credit cards, and gave them to Harlan."

"I told Harlan that Jerome wanted him to make a trail with them so the police or his scoundrel of a father could never find him."

"The night you killed Harlan, I suppose he'd told you he wasn't going to take the rap, that he intended to tell me exactly what had happened."

"I didn't mean to kill him either, just to talk him into leaving town. Harlan caused his own death. He came at me like a madman. I was only trying to protect myself."

"You got to thinking you might have missed removing some of your fingerprints," McQuede said, "and so that's why you showed up at the crime scene, so I would think they were left there innocently." McQuede turned to stare at him. "Maybe I could understand killing someone in a fight, but you planned to murder Loris in cold blood."

"That's not what I wanted either. I loved her! I asked her to marry me. She had the audacity to reject me, just as they all did back in high school." A tinge of pride crept into his voice. "I kidnapped her and brought her out to this lake she's so sentimental about. Before I came to your office, I broke into her place. I knew you'd think I did it searching for her. I wrote that note myself and took her gun. I almost succeeded. Clever, wasn't it? Like the way I fooled you over that blackmail money. I had to break into Fenton's and get that incriminating picture. So you would never suspect it existed, I used that blackmail scheme as a ploy."

McQuede thought again of the judgmental way Sammy Ratone criticized crimes of which he was not personally guilty. Ganner, though, had a different slant; he was guilty of them all and justified them regardless. And it had begun with killing an old chum for the cash in his wallet.

Ganner sank into a self-pitying silence. Good thing he pitied himself, McQuede thought, for McQuede didn't feel the slightest compassion for him. An ironic and terrible picture rose in McQuede's mind, of Ganner, with his so-called success, day after day walking through the high school, across the gym floor over the place where he had buried Jerome Slade.

McQuede entered the office to find Sid Carlisle talking to Heather and Fredrick Preston. "I just told them we got the blackmail money back. Where have you been, anyway?"

"At the hospital," McQuede said. "Bruce Fenton will make a full recovery."

"I thought he was dead," Heather burst out.

"I only made Ganner think he had killed him so he wouldn't shoot us all. Here's the story I got from Fenton. He trailed me out to the lake for your sake, Ms. Kenwell. He was going to tell me that he had watched you all evening the night of the dance and would testify that you didn't kill Jerome."

"What did he think I'd be doing out at that old lake?"

"Hiding from me. He thought I was chasing you and that I was going to arrest you."

"Why would he think that . . . oh, never mind. He's always been a little crazy."

McQuede crossed to his desk and handed Heather a manila envelope. "We found these in Ev Ganner's house. The photos and negatives are all in here. I think Fenton has learned his lesson."

"You know what I'm going to do? I'm going to take

them home and burn them. I'm so relieved knowing they won't turn up to destroy my campaign."

"Our campaign," Preston corrected. "I've signed on as her manager." He smiled, an overly self-satisfied smile like those of the rich and famous, and said a little condescendingly, "We want to thank you, Sheriff, for everything you've done."

McQuede watched Preston put his arm around Heather's shoulder as they walked away. He was glad that they had gotten back together. The two deserved each other. He only wished his own romance would end that well.

McQuede reached for his jacket, saying, "I've got to pick up Loris' painting."

"Ganner burned the frame, but he couldn't bring himself to destroy Carlo's valuable work," Sid remarked. "Lucky for her. I found it rolled up and hidden in his basement along with the blackmail money and the photos."

"The blackmail and the painting theft were mostly to throw us off the track, but I suppose Ganner wasn't opposed to hanging on to easy money."

"I would have suspected him sooner, but I was focusing on Ruger and Sammy Ratone," Sid said. "I spoke to the old, retired sheriff, who told me no matter how hard he tried, he could never make a case against either of them."

"It won't be long," McQuede returned, "Now that Sammy owns The Drifter, we're bound to catch them red-handed—at something."

McQuede stepped back to admire his handiwork, proud that the oak frame he'd bought for Loris complimented the painting. He tilted his head. "Is it just my imagination, or is it still leaning a little to the side?"

"I think you've got it now," Loris said. "This Carlo means so much to me." She looked at McQuede approvingly. "Thanks to you, I've got it back."

"You deserve to, after the time you've had."

"Jeff, remember when I told you I had a theory about who killed Jerome? Bruce had given me copies of his photos, and one day I was sorting through them. I was surprised to find a picture Bruce had taken of Heather meeting Jerome the night of the dance. At the time, I thought Heather was guilty, so I took the print to Bruce to be enlarged, thinking it would contain some clue."

"Then you called Bruce telling him you were coming down to the studio to pick it up."

"Yes," Loris said. "But as I was getting into my car, I was attacked. And that's why I thought Bruce was guilty."

"Then you didn't once suspect Ev Ganner."

Loris said sadly, "Ev has always been my friend. I still can't believe he murdered Jerome." She paused, immersed in memories. "All these years I thought that Jerome jilted me, the same way he had Heather. Year after year, I imagined him singing, on the verge of becoming famous. That's what Jerome wanted most, more than he wanted either Heather or me."

"Jerome and Harlan were linked to a string of robberies," McQuede told her. "Jerome thought he was soon to be charged with them, and that's why he wanted to leave Black Mountain. No doubt he intended to come back for you."

Loris brightened a little. "Jerome was guilty of many things, but not of deserting me." She paused, thoughtfully, then as if mourning the death of a fantasy, added, "Jerome was not only a thief, but he accepted Fredrick's bribe—even though he had no intention of leaving here with Heather."

A frail excuse for a man, McQuede thought, at the beck and call of money. McQuede suddenly recalled how Sammy Ratone had accused him of seeing only good and evil, not the big gray areas in between.

What did Sammy Ratone expect? McQuede had spent his life sorting the good guys from the bad guys. He'd solved this case because he hadn't been thrown off track by seas of gray. He had rescued Loris because in his heart he'd never stopped seeing her as innocent.

Loris gazed at the painting, then at him. She looked so beautiful.

McQuede returned her smile, feeling content and happy. He guessed he'd just keep on seeing the world in black and white.

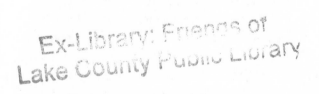